The Parrot Told Me

ALSO BY

Rachael Rawlings

———————

Dearly Departed

The Parrot Told Me

Rachael Rawlings

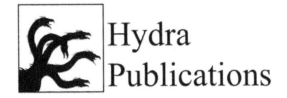
Hydra Publications

Copyright © 2014 by Tony Acree
All rights reserved.

This book or any portion thereof
may not be reproduced or used in any manner whatsoever
without the express written permission of the publisher
except for the use of brief quotations in a book review.

Printed in the United States of America

ISBN: 0996086757
ISBN-13: 978-0-9960867-5-2

Hydra Publications
1310 Meadowridge Trail
Goshen, KY 40026

www.hydrapublications.com

DEDICATION

This one is to my parents, who introduced me to the crazy world of parrots. Thanks for the support, the encouragement, the loyalty, and the firm foundation of faith that you have shown every day.

Chapter 1

"Are you my baby bird?" The question was pronounced in a high pitched, strangely raspy voice.

Camille turned a page and concentrated on the printed words.

"Are you my baby bird?" The voice insisted, accompanied by a loud ringing and the discordant sound of metal against metal.

"Hey, Simon," Camille called back, closing her book.

"Baby bird," the voice returned. "Pasta time?"

Camille laughed and propped her bare feet on the antique trunk before her. The rough wood gave slightly beneath the weight and creaked in protest.

A copy of the creak sounded from the dining room. A moment later, it sounded again, this time followed by a piercing whistle.

"It's not time to eat yet, boy." Camille flipped her novel to the couch and rubbed her hand over her eyes.

"Pasta time?"

Camille stood and slowly stretched. The fire was too cozy. Her sagging couch, slip-covered a bright red, was as comfortable as a big overstuffed feather bed. A vanilla candle guttering in a pool of sweet scented wax cast its glow over her shabby room, turning scuffed wood into smooth veneer and disguising the tatters and bald patches on the upholstery.

Through the kitchen door, she could see her newest roommate pacing. Simon was a trifle scruffy as well, his charcoal grey feathers ruffled and battered, but improving. He had begun to gain weight back and he no longer flared with anger when someone passed through the doorway.

Camille shook her head and slipped across the room.

"How about a little music?" she asked, switching on Vivaldi's Four Seasons. The sound filtered from the speakers, crystal clear, lovely.

The pacing stopped; the clang of the bell was silenced as the

The Parrot Told Me

sensitive creature bent his head to absorb the comfort of the sound, his figure reflected in the dark glass of the window. A bird that loved classical music. How unique.

Camille took her seat again, choosing a magazine from the stack on the top of the trunk. She flipped open the glossy pages, too distracted to concentrate on her novel. There was something inherently splendid about sitting in the half-light, the vanilla scented air rushing on warm drafts, the music washing over her like a salve.

"What the hell?" This time the voice was different, feminine, spooky. The voice of a dead woman.

Camille caught her breath.

"Just here for a visit." The voice returned an octave lower, a man.

"Look, I don't want to discuss it." The first voice again, but different. She didn't sound angry anymore, but cautious maybe.

"Baby." A man's voice.

Then there was a long pause, a pregnant silence filled only by the music.

"Let me go." It was the female voice again, but higher, afraid.

The cacophony of sounds that followed were signs of the furious struggle, then an unearthly howl, a bird voice of fury as the music shut off, a few seconds of silence before the next track began.

Camille stumbled to her feet, the magazine sliding to the floor unheeded. Her heart was hammering in her ears as the noise ceased an insistent clanging melting into silence.

"Oh, poor bird," the lonely creature crooned, once again in his raspy voice. "Poor Simon."

With her hand at her chest, sheltering her stuttering heart, she leaned forward and looked in the dining room again. Simon was in the back of his cage, perched at his favorite spot, huddled against the walls. His left foot was raised, his long parrot claws gently massaging his own neck. A parrot's self-comfort.

~*~

Leonard Hawkins was something of an old man's name in Camille's opinion, which was the reason her first introduction to Leonard was such a shock.

Leo was like no other man that she had ever met. His face was long and lean, his skin fashionably tanned to an overall golden color. His hair, a riot of blond and ash, stood in porcupine quills all over his perfectly sculptured head. He was breathtaking in his male beauty, startling in his wit, and her best friend.

When he noticed her sneaking in late the third day in a row, his smile was bright and, ever so slightly, devious.

"Good morning, Sunshine," he said in a smooth undertone, his smile flashing white with incredibly straight teeth.

She gave an exasperated sigh. "Leo, if you insist on speaking to me this early in the morning, the least you could do is keep that smile off your face."

"Nice attitude," he huffed, turning back to his humming computer. When she looked back at him he had a half smile playing on his lips. As he gave her a side glance, he asked slyly, "How long until you're decent?"

She spun back toward him, hands on her hips. "Oh, for heaven's sake. Go get me some coffee, and maybe I'll recover."

He actually whistled as he strolled into the back office, returning with a brimming cup of perfectly sweetened coffee and a bagel. He handed her the offering silently, but with a slight mocking bow.

"So late night out? New guy?"

She sighed again and took a long sip of the warm drink. "You know more about my love life than I do. I think it's pretty unlikely that in the last 24 hours I found a fabulous catch. Besides, after that last disastrous date, I'm thinking of becoming a nun."

"Sister Cammy. Now that's sweet," he murmured grinning.

"Um," she said, switching on her terminal and watching the screen blink in a flurry of codes and numbers. "But I did have something interesting happen to me."

"Do tell," he said, bending to sort out incoming books onto the stacking cart.

"Well, you remember Simon?" she began, pausing until he nodded a trifle impatiently. "He was talking last night—"

"Wait," Leo interrupted, straightening. "Not to be presumptuous, but we're not discussing your love life anymore." At Camille's grimace, he attempted to wipe the slightly indulgent smile off of his mobile face.

The Parrot Told Me

"Now is this the bird that you got from your neighbor?"

"Dead neighbor," she amended slightly cool.

"Young, dead, sexy neighbor."

"How do you know? Did you ever see her?" Camille asked, her eyebrows rising to meet the errant lock of ebony hair.

"Of course," he responded in an offended tone. "I checked her out when she was picking up her mail. She gave me that look. I looked back, just like any normal male. That's how I knew who she was when you mentioned her untimely demise. She was in 304, just above you, right?"

"Yeah, close," Camille replied slowly. "And what look are you referring to?"

He dipped his head and peered at Camille from beneath perfectly arched brows. "The look that you seem to have forgotten after the long drought of no date land."

"I could have dates if I chose," Camille responded frowning. "I just choose not to date your questionable friends, or the slime that thrives at those techno dives you call fun." She frowned slightly. "Besides, don't you think it's kind of creepy talking about someone who's dead in those terms? Sexy?"

"Touché," Leo said with a slightly superior smile. "But remember, men have panted over Monroe for years, and she's certainly past tense."

Camille huffed a response and crossed her arms over her chest. She wondered for the millionth time how she had ended up with him as her best friend and confidant. It wasn't as though they had loads in common. He had an active social life, a penchant for choosing the most undesirable men as friends, and the worst taste in movies. But he did have something that she valued above all others. He was strong and loyal and he loved her unconditionally.

"Okay, so I'll give you some credit. You do know something about women."

"I try," he said grinning. "Now I'll be merciful and let you talk about your pet."

"Not my pet. He was hers. And he still is. He really misses her." She stopped speaking when his face revealed his disbelief, an expression she was growing to dislike intensely. "I can tell he's still in mourning."

10

She explained patiently. "He speaks in her voice all the time."

"We are talking about that ratty parrot in your kitchen, right?"

Camille frowned and put her fists on her hips, a clear sign of impatience.

"Okay, fine, I'll grant you, that must be eerie," Leo remarked, slightly impressed. "But how well did you really know her?" Camille grimaced as she turned away from the computer screen. Although she could count the number of conversations she had had with her deceased neighbor on one hand, she couldn't forget the voice. It was one of those distinct sounds that stuck with you. Monica had been born somewhere in the far south, and even in Kentucky, her drawl had been easy to pick out. Combine that with a rather husky vocal quality, and Monica had a sweet sensual sound that was perfect for bluegrass music and barefoot discussions around the open fire. Not that Camille was ever aware of Monica taking up any of those hobbies. The music emanating from the floor above tended toward hard rock, and the visitors were often the tragic, gothic type.

"Trust me, it was her voice," Camille said darkly.

"So what about the bird bothers you?" Leo asked, pulling Camille from her reverie.

"I'm getting to it," Camille responded. "Last night, Simon was talking like he usually does—"

"And that is?" Leo interrupted.

Camille sighed. Leo was a great guy, truly, but he had been known to tune out during conversations, all the while maintaining a credible smile and nodding at all the right places.

"I've told you about him," she said patiently, perching on her stool. "He's an African Grey parrot, and most of them have an unbelievable vocabulary. He talks, sings songs, and makes all kind of sound effect noises."

"I do remember you telling me about those," Leo said, glancing to the door when a patron strolled in.

"If you'd stop by once in a while you could meet him," Camille said, sending him a pointed look.

"My place has better ambiance."

"A bigger TV, you mean," she corrected.

"Your opinion," he replied, waving carelessly.

The Parrot Told Me

"Well, anyway, Simon has been with me for almost a month now, and he's really starting to get his speech back." Camille paused and watched while an older woman strolled by, several books tucked under her arm. Camille nodded at the woman and waited until she had ducked behind the shelves before continuing.

"Simon stopped talking when Monica died," Camille explained. "Parrots are very sensitive, and a death like that can be devastating. He went into an all-out depression. He was ripping his feathers out and not eating his food." Camille shuddered when she recalled the terrible shape the bird had been in. "I wasn't sure if he was going to make it through the first week, and then all of the sudden, he snapped out of it. He started talking and eating again, paying attention to me and the other critters."

"Your charm, I'm sure," Leo quipped.

"Right," Camille replied, making a face. "Anyway, he talks most of the time when I'm in the other room."

"Shy?"

Camille ignored the comment. "Last night he started talking like he usually does, begging for food mostly. Each bird learns a repertoire of statements that they like to use."

"Does he know you don't cook?" Leo interrupted.

"He's not picky, unlike some people I might mention."

Leo let the comment slide, but Camille knew he was mostly right. She was a terrible cook, didn't like to cook, and therefore avoided it.

"Anyway, he started this dialogue. It was the strangest thing." Camille briefly reiterated the conversation, describing the bird's obvious agitation.

"I know where this is leading," Leo muttered, easing from his stool and pushing away from the counter. "Now you've got a wild hair about this woman and how she died."

"Not really," Camille said defensively.

"Right," Leo replied, grinning. "Did it ever occur to you that the dialogue you heard might be from TV, a movie, or something?"

"Of course," Camille snapped. "But look at it this way. It usually takes deliberate training and repeating something many times for a bird to learn speech. Do you really think she repeated a section of a movie for the bird to learn?"

"You just argued yourself out of your own theory," Leo

countered. "If you need repetition for the bird to learn, then how would he recall a live conversation?"

"If the conversation had enough emotion, or meaning, he might have recalled it on his own," Camille said, leaning closer. "I've heard of birds hearing a sound or word that they really like and remembering it after just one time."

Leo frowned. "Alright, say I give you that one as a possibility. But you still don't know how Monica died, do you? Isn't this all speculation?" He leaned against the counter and crossed his arms over his chest. "She probably died of natural causes."

"A healthy woman of thirty or so dying suddenly of natural causes?"

"It happens."

"Not that often."

"Okay, car accident, drug overdose, suicide. There are a lot of possibilities." Leo looked at Camille with a more serious expression on his face. "I don't want this to turn into a crusade."

"It won't," Camille said flatly. With a shrug, and a swift shake of her head she looked him straight in his eyes. "Really, Leo, it won't. No joke."

Leo raised his eyebrows in that expression that she hated so well. With a sniff, she turned to the tightly stacked cart of books and pushed it out from behind the desk. For her, the conversation was over, and she'd be damned if she brought up the subject again. At least, not until she found some evidence to back up her emerging theory.

~*~

The next week brought more headaches than Camille had anticipated and even with Leo's support, she ended up spending long hours working in the closed bookstore. The matter of Monica's death took second chair as she closed herself in her office. Tax season was fast approaching and much of her spare time was spent gathering paperwork to take to the accountant's office.

An extra evening or two went to reorganizing her desk and file cabinet, as she plowed through the mountains of paperwork that she had accumulated over the Christmas Holidays. On her way home on Friday,

The Parrot Told Me

she stopped to run by the post office before Leo came to pick her up for dinner. The sky was a dull smoky grey yielding a spitting mix of rain, sleet, and snow that was so typical for the region and time of year. But the dimness suited Camille's mood because she was soured from the constant pressure of owning her own business, no matter how much she actually loved the bookstore.

Leo had been very little help in lightening her mood at closing. After scolding her for not eating enough and not calling her mother back promptly, he had settled into full big brother mode and lectured her about her lack of social life.

"If you went out every once in a while you wouldn't get so obsessed with the item of the day. First it's the shop, then it's that damn bird, and now I bet your thinking of your neighbor. You've got that look in your eye."

Leo's observations, however rude, were very true and brought on a wealth of questions that Camille insisted must be answered. If something happened, she wanted to know why and how. If a light went out, a tree fell, a river changed its path, and she wanted to know the reason. She had to discover the truths behind all of life's mysteries. It was the order and pattern of the universe that drove her, fascinated her. And the human condition was no exception.

And what had happened to her neighbor, while not affecting Camille's life that directly, had an impact. And despite some tragedies that she had lived through, her neighbor's death was significant. Leo might scoff, but after all, what had happened to Monica? One day she was living, working, making due with her time, and the next day, gone. There had been only a brief mention of her death in the obituaries, and Camille, who had never had much of a relationship with any of her neighbors, had had only a nodding acquaintance with Monica. Her death, as tragic as it had been, wouldn't have caused but a ripple in Camille's day to day life had it not been for Simon.

Back to Simon. It all seemed to be intricately associated with the pitiful neurotic bird and his astounding memory.

In the beginning, no one had been more surprised than Camille when her landlady had called her up on the telephone and scolded her for not returning the messages left on her answering machine. Camille had sputtered a reply, chagrined because she had known the outdated machine was unreliable at best.

Mrs. Nan Patterson was not one to be ignored, and Camille had immediately followed her directions and hurried to the first floor apartment that Mrs. Patterson called her own.

Camille had only been there once before at moving time, and then she had gotten no further than the fussy front room. Mrs. Patterson was a tyrant for privacy, and guarded hers like a Leprechaun over a cauldron brimming with gold.

On that occasion when Camille was brand new to the building, she had stood, shifting from foot to foot, as Mrs. Patterson had gone in search of rental papers that she needed Camille to sign. It had been uncomfortable and she could almost feel her skin crawling as she gazed about the room, feeling the painted eyes of dozens of dolls pinning her to the papered wall. They were literally everywhere, sitting upright on shelves, standing guard on in tables, and tucked between sofa cushions.

No one had warned her that Nan Patterson collected dolls. Why had no one warned her?

With a hunted looked, Camille had backed away from the heavy brocade chair and frilled pillow boasting an occupant dressed in an antique lace wedding dress, and plastered her back against the door. The exit. Time stretched like chewing gum in a child's fingers, and Camille felt fine beads of sweat bloom on her upper lip and along her hairline.

She barely remembered the papers or what she signed, standing with her back to the nightmare room and her hand drawing a parody of her signature as she leaned against the door.

But the next time she went in response to the phone call, she had been ushered impatiently past the pastel kingdom and into the kitchen.

That was when she first met Simon.

~*~

"He's yours," her landlady had stated, pulling Camille out of her reverie. "Take him," she said, gesturing to the huge wrought iron cage housing a rather ratty looking bird.

"Is that?" Camille's voice left her in a squeak.

"It's Simon. Miss Gibs wanted you to have him."

"Monica? She wanted me to take him?" Camille asked stupidly.

The Parrot Told Me

"That is what the cousin said. Take him." Mrs. Patterson turned impatiently from Camille. "I have an appointment in 15 minutes."

Camille barely had time to glance around at the faded linoleum and cracked countertops before she was literally shoved out the door, the wheeled cage shuttering on the uneven floor. The cage was a huge monster, but it did move, all the while the terrified occupant huddled in the corner and growled in a low, fierce voice. Camille had to be impressed when the creature hurled himself at the cage wall as they passed the parlor of dolls, his emotions mirroring her own. And with that, they were forcefully ejected into the hallway and the door closed behind them, leaving Camille and the bird eyeing each other wearily.

The elevator ride had been a singularly unpleasant experience, the odor of a cage full of bird droppings almost suffocating in the tiny space. The elevator wheezed to a stop at Camille's floor, and she shoved the cage into the hallway, pausing to stare at the bird again. He looked back, what feathers he retained ruffled and overblown. Then he issued a wild, ear piercing whistle and fluttered to a top perch. With a muttered "What the hell," Camille steered him into her apartment and closed the door.

And with that, Camille was linked forever with Monica Gibs untimely death.

Chapter 2

Now she knew that she wasn't going to have much time. Leo was coming, and she really needed to finish her errand if she was going to be back in her apartment on time. With a low groan, Camille climbed the last few steps to the first floor and went toward the front door to grab her personal mail. She needed an excuse, and this one was as good as any. With hands full of catalogues and credit card offers, she turned back down the hall.

She wanted nothing more than to climb back up the stairs and retreat into her own apartment. But she couldn't, wouldn't, until she had pried a bit of truth out of her closed mouthed landlady. Or died trying.

The rings on her fingers, five in all, glinted when she rapped her fist against the polished wood of the door. Hastily, she pulled her hand down and palmed four of the rings, stuffing them in her jeans pocket. She quickly ran her fingers through her hair, attempting to smooth her choppy locks into something resembling a style.

The door popped open before Camille could knock again and she stepped back when her landlady appeared in the doorway.

"Yes?" It wasn't a pleasant tone, to be sure.

Camille pasted a smile on her face and clasped her hands before her to stop their fidgeting.

"I, um, was checking my mail when I noticed the lock was a little hinky," Camille improvised, her face flushing.

"And?"

"Well, I hate to think it isn't working right. You know, someone might be able to get in..." Her voice sank into silence at the blank expression on the other woman's face. But then, Mrs. Patterson's expression rarely became animated. When she spoke, the lines on her face seemed to lift and tighten, not in a smile but a grimace. Her sharp green eyes peered at Camille over outdated half glasses balanced on a bony nose.

The Parrot Told Me

"You are worried someone might get into your mailbox?" Mrs. Patterson's voice was plainly scornful and Camille could see now how ridiculous the claim was. A locked building. Camille herself had very little of value.

Mrs. Patterson continued to study Camille and with one pale naked hand, drew the glasses from her nose and let them fall against the meager mounds of her breasts.

"I don't know." Camille looked uncomfortably down the narrow, high ceiling hallway.

"Fine. I'll take care of it."

"Well, I don't want to cause any big fuss," Camille said quickly. "In fact, I thought that I might, to make things simple, just borrow another box for a while."

Mrs. Patterson's eyes were blank and unreadable.

"There is an empty box, isn't there?" Camille asked, tucking her hands deeper in her pockets.

"Of course, number 304."

"I could just put my number on it," Camille continued quickly. "Unless there is someone moving in who needs the box?"

Mrs. Patterson edged further into the hallway, forcing Camille to back away as well.

"The apartment is still empty," the older woman said flatly, glancing down the hall.

"It was such a shame," Camille stated tentatively. "Monica was so young to die so tragically."

Mrs. Patterson's lips narrowed with something like distaste. "It is not an accident I like to discuss," she said, her tone almost angry.

"I'm sorry," Camille stuttered, startled at the chill rising in the other woman's eyes. "I didn't realize you were so close."

"Please," Mrs. Patterson said, her voice pitched low. "I don't want the others to hear about the accident, and I don't want our name or reputation smirched."

"Our name?" Camille asked, baffled. "You mean this apartment building?"

The expression on Mrs. Patterson's face grew tighter, her thin lips clinched so that they almost disappeared in her parchment white face.

"I'll take care of your lock immediately. There will be no need to move your box." She withdrew into her rooms and shut the door so quickly that Camille felt the rush of air.

"Now that was interesting," Camille murmured to herself, heading back up to her second floor apartment. It wasn't as though she had expected a cozy gossip session, complete with oatmeal raisin cookies and hot tea. But the utter secrecy was a little on the extreme. Granted, it might not be the perfect way to advertise a building or apartment to lease. Some may have real qualms about moving into a place recently vacated by a corpse. But on the other hand, as small as Lexington was, it was a college town and a decent apartment was often hard to find. Especially one that was situated in an historic building like this one which had been kept in good condition over the years.

Camille paused at the doorway of her apartment. She felt a strange chill, the fine hairs rising at the back of her neck and her scalp tightening in response. She looked both ways down the hallway. Nothing. The merciless lighting revealed stark white walls and tough woven rugs laid over hardwood. The string of doors, six in all, stretched out in either direction. The red exit sign cast a faint red reflection on the slick painted wall behind.

All doors were shut tight, no peepers peering from behind door frames. Then why did she feel as though someone was watching?

Briskly she rubbed her arms and scanned the hall once final time. She had thought about rushing upstairs to check out Monica's apartment. She wanted, no, was dying to see the inside of that closed apartment. It was her nature to be impulsive and to follow that impulse. But for once, good sense prevailed, or perhaps it was plain old save your own hide fear. Instead she retreated inside her own rooms, content to huddle under a handmade quilt and plot her next move.

~*~

When Leo arrived in the hallway to pick her up for dinner a half hour later, she chuckled out loud. His puzzlement was evident on his face, but she had little sympathy. There were three doors cracked open, each, she was sure, hiding a female behind the thick panels.

Leo attracted women like a picnic attracted ants. He couldn't help

The Parrot Told Me

it, Camille knew, although his meticulous attention to his appearance did little to dissuade his feminine admirers.

One of the braver women, Chloe, from across the hall, had the audacity, or perhaps just the lacked social skills, to prop her door open and stroll out with no pretense.

"Camille, hey," she called in a shrill voice, piercing enough to make Camille wince at the sound. She moved with experience on high heels, and her tight jeans hugged her thin frame.

"Chloe," Camille returned cautiously.

Leo stood aside, smiling politely.

"So how's your new pet?" Chloe asked, stepping into the hall and smiling falsely with hot pink painted lips.

Camille stared at her in surprise, not quick enough to keep her emotions off of her face.

"I heard you ended up with Monica's bird. Such an unusual pet."

"Um, yes," Camille said, wondering briefly where that information had come from.

"Such a tragedy," Chloe continued. "To die so young and in such a way." She traced one long pink nail down the front of her tight tee-shirt, pausing to tug on a silver chain that looped twice around her slender neck.

Camille looked at Leo and he glanced back, his eyebrows raised. She wasn't sure if his expression had more to do with Chloe's blatant come on, or her knowledge of the accident. Camille had not even thought that Chloe would have heard the details of Monica's death. Not when Mrs. Patterson was deliberately trying to suppress the information. But apparently the power of the grapevine was even more formidable than Mrs. Patterson's wicked glare.

"It was a tragedy," Camille agreed, unwilling to reveal her ignorance about the subject.

Leo, however had no such compunction. With a smile that would mesmerize any unsuspecting female, he turned to the hapless Chloe.

"I hadn't heard," he said, his voice deep with just a touch of sensuality. "What did happen to Monica?"

"Oh," Chloe exclaimed, clearly delighted to be able to share this gristly information with an attractive male. "Well our landlady found her," she explained, drawing closer to Leo. She hesitated and glanced down the hall, her face intense as though she were revealing some terrible secret. "She was in the bathtub. She was naked, well of course she was," Chloe tittered behind her fingertips, "but anyway, she was surrounded by," a slight pause for dramatic effect, "candles."

Now Camille herself relished a long hot bath with scented candles and a good glass of wine every once in a while, and saw nothing deviant in that behavior. As a matter of fact, she had strong suspicions that Chloe's own tastes ran to an even more risky sort of entertainment. So the statement, accompanied by the sly look and sense of intimacy, left Camille feeling a little skeptical.

Leo, apparently, had no such hesitation and cocked his head in apparent fascination. "Really," he prodded.

"She was electrocuted." Chloe paused, leaning back with a satisfied smile as though she had just successfully told a fairytale to a bunch of spellbound kindergarteners.

"Oh," Leo said slowly. "How?"

Camille was beginning to feel a little guilty, speaking of the dead woman in such a way, and contemplated going back into her apartment in protest. But this was what she had wanted to know, needed to know, if she were to ever get resolution.

"It was the radio. All that loud rock music. You could hear it all the way down the hall upstairs, and sometimes even down here." She scrunched her nose in what Camille was sure she considered a charming way. "The radio just," a blithe hand gesture, "tumbled in the tub. And zip, dead."

Camille suppressed her words until they were safely in her apartment, the door securely locked.

"Ha," she said, thrusting a finger in Leo's face. "I'm not going to say I told you so but..."

"I thought you weren't going to say it."

"I'm not. Not really. The point is, Monica didn't just die in a car accident or of a brain aneurism."

"She was electrocuted having a bubble bath. It's sad, Camille, but not proof of any foul play." He paused, a smile curling the corners of his mouth. "Get it, fowl play?"

"Ha," Camille said again, humorlessly. "I know it doesn't prove anything, but isn't it like, reasonable doubt or something?"

The Parrot Told Me

He ran a hand through his spiked hair, his fingers barely ruffling his stiff locks.

"Okay, Perry Mason. What do you intend to do about it? Have the bird go State's evidence? He's a bird, for God's sake, and you haven't any proof that he wasn't quoting her favorite movie."

"Yet," Camille said calmly. "I haven't any proof yet."

Chapter 3

And how do I get proof? Camille lay back on her bed, one finger tracing the intricate pattern of her canopy which was draped from bed post to bed post. How did one go about proving a murder when all they had heard was the second hand mutterings of a bird on the edge?

She sat up and tugged her blouse down, tucking it neatly into her slightly worn jeans. The blouse was a vibrant lime green, the same color as her toenails. She smiled wryly. Those, at least, would be hidden in her short boots. Leo was opening today so she had roughly three hours to waste. She intended to make use of that time to further her cause.

She frowned at her reflection in the mirror. Was she taking this thing too far? She paused in front of the mirror and examined her reflected eyes. She wasn't getting enough sleep and the dreams had returned with a vengeance. She was a shade too pale, but her skin had always tended toward the milk white. The terrible dye job she had gotten three weeks ago was beginning to grow out and her mahogany roots streaked down her part.

"Crap," she muttered. She applied a dab of red to her lips and stepped back. She debated over the string of five earrings that graced her right ear and removed three to match the left. The shirt was hopeless, too wrinkled and a shade too tight, but it would have to do.

"Now if I were going to get into an apartment, how would I do that?" Her reflection gave no answers.

In the kitchen, she checked on Simon as well as her own cockatiel, Casey. The birds' uneasy alliance had held for several weeks, but Camille was careful not to release them at the same time or let Casey climb on Simon's cage. She didn't want a bird with a few less toes or the vet bills that would accompany any avian accidents.

Simone eyed her silently as she paused before his cage. "Who would have the keys?" she asked the bird as he climbed slowly to the door and emitted a low, mournful whistle. "Leo has my apartment key,

The Parrot Told Me

and mom and dad, and the neighbor," she murmured. She bit her lip as she considered the options. She didn't know much about friends or family that Monica might have been close too, but she certainly had neighbors. But she couldn't just go knocking to see if anyone had a set of keys to Monica's apartment, nor could she drop a note in a few mailboxes to see if she got a bite. Mrs. Patterson's grim visage rose in her mind and she grimaced. If her landlady found about any of those type activities, Camille would be looking for a new home.

She looked at Simon a moment longer as though she might find an answer in his pearl grey eyes. He emitted a sharp whistle and ducked his head in a nodding bob.

"Okay, I'm going," Camille said frowning. She grabbed her keys from the basket by the door and engaged the lock. Through the door she heard the bird speaking, calling "Goodbye, Sweetie," in Monica's unmistakable tones. The sound drove her up the stairs to the next floor, the hair on the back of her neck prickling unpleasantly.

The hallway upstairs was similar to her own. The building had long been used as an apartment and each of the five floors were repeats of one another. It made a simple task to find the dead woman's door in the silent hallway.

Camille paused outside, afraid almost to touch the grained surface of the door. Drat, but it was quiet. Like a tomb. The wall sconces, perfectly appropriate in their glass and brass splendor, were sadly lacking with bulbs blown. The window too seemed to be conspiring for a glooming atmosphere with only stingy glow seeping through the heavy curtains.

A shiver snuck up Camille's spine and she turned back toward the stirs. Stupid, stupid! What was she thinking? If there was a murder in her building, it stood to reason that there would also be a murderer. And who was she to get involved in this? The closest she had been to intrigue in the last several years had been the mystery section at the bookstore.

A figure appeared at the top of the steps, tall and growing taller.

An unconscious explicative slipped from Camille's lips and she dug in her pocket to wrap her fingers around her keys.

The figure was more visible now. A man, middle aged or younger, rough hewn and slightly slovenly, moved with an uneven tread.

24

"What do you want?"

His voice was as rough as his unshaven face, his eyes hidden behind tinted lenses that were unnecessary in the dimly lit hall.

"What?" Camille was proud that her voice was even and slightly aloof, although the response certainly wasn't her wittiest. Camille took one small step back, her eyes glancing nervously down the hall.

"You're standing outside of my door," he responded, his voice full of exaggerated patience. "What are you doing here?"

Camille automatically turned and looked at the door at her elbow. She had unconsciously moved toward the stairs in her discomfort and stood in front of 304, the apartment just above her own. Her relief was inexplicable.

"I, um, didn't mean..." She stopped and pulled out her keys, crossing her arms protectively. "I was just looking for one of Monica's neighbors. I need keys to get in her apartment."

It was hard to read his expression, masked by the whiskers and glasses, but body language revealed much. The subtle stiffening of his shoulders and the way he cocked his head made Camille more nervous than before. He was easily 6'4 and his shoulders stretched his corduroy jacket to its rather worn seams. When he looked behind her toward Monica's closed door, Camille grew suspicious about his relationship with his deceased neighbor.

"Why do you need in Monica's apartment?"

"I have her bird, Simon. He's still looking really bad and the vet said he needed some familiar things from his old home." Camille was proud of her own improvising. "I need to find out what food he was on, what toys he liked, all of that."

"We are talking about the bird?"

Camille almost laughed. The man's stance had relaxed significantly and he seemed more incredulous than angry.

"Yes. Monica left him to me. I've been trying to take care of him, but he doesn't look well."

"I don't know if I should hand over the key just like that," he said frowning. "I think you should talk to Mrs. Patterson." He looked as though he were ready to dismiss her that easily.

Camille ducked her head, her mind running and scattering through possible excuses. "I checked," she blurted. "She's out. And

The Parrot Told Me

frankly, I didn't want to bother her." At least the last part was true, and she just hoped he wouldn't check on her excuse. "I'm Camille, by the way." She tried to look charming.

He muttered an expletive. He pulled off his glasses and stuffed them in a jacket pocket. His hands were darkly stained with black under the nails and printing his fingertips. His eyes, without the dark glasses, were a blood shot pale blue green, his eyebrows dark slashes of aggravation. A battered baseball cap, blue and dingy white, shaded his forehead and covered his hair. "Max Danbury," he said curtly. "I just got off 15 hours, I can't think."

"I'll be very quick," Camille reassured him, sensing his weakening. She was smugly pleased with herself, not only had she lucked into the right neighbor, but this one was almost willing to help her.

"Can you come back in the afternoon? I'll have had some rest and can help you out then."

Camille shifted her feet, angling toward the closed apartment door. "I really can't," she responded. "I have to be at work in a few hours, so this is will be my only opportunity for a while."

He made a low sound, somewhere between a grunt and a growl.

"Why couldn't you have contacted Mara? She would know more about what the bird needed," he grumbled.

"Mara?"

"Mara something, I think, Monica's best friend. She was as close to Monica as anyone." He ran one ling fingered hand across his unshaven jaw and yanked the cap from his head. His dark hair was pressed against his head in a less than attractive style. It was much longer than she had first thought and he kept it back in an elastic band at his nape. He impatiently brushed a few stray strands back with his grimy palm and replaced the cap. His blood shot eyes were sharp and assessing; the grunt muttered in a low and frustrated voice.

"I'm sorry to be a bother, but I wanted to get Simon's things before they cleaned out the apartment. I promise I won't disturb anything else."

He heaved a sigh and Camille wondered again if any of his hesitation stemmed from a relationship Monica and he had shared.

"Look," he said reluctantly. "I'll let you in, but you've got to come back and return the key. Mrs. Patterson knows that I have the only copy, and she'll want it back." He paused, his expression unreadable, "and don't take anything." Camille's mouth dropped open in protest but he had already turned back into the apartment. He emerged a few moments later with a key dangling from a pair of miniature pink fuzzy dice.

"I'll have them back in just a second," Camille promised. She waited until his door closed before stepping next door to try the key. Her pumping heart sounded uncomfortably fast in her ears. She wondered briefly if it were possible to pass out just from stress. She really didn't want to open the door. She had a sudden flash of her sister's bedroom at their parent's home, pristine and untouched. It made her faintly nauseous. Her own actions suddenly seemed insane. Why was she doing this? Because of the bird? Because of Monica? Worse, could Leo be right and could it be because of her sister?

She shook her head and set her jaw unconsciously. The key turned and she pushed to door ajar. With sure steps she entered the room and closed the door firmly yet quietly behind her. Then she locked it, just because it felt like the right thing to do.

All the apartments in the building had the same basic floor plan, but it was incredible how different this space was from her own. The walls were painted vibrant sherbet colors such as lime green and neon orange with yellow accents on woodwork.

Camille stepped around a satin covered love-seat, running her fingers along the slick black fabric. A red throw was carelessly bunched in the corner. Its sinuous curves and slick sheen made it look like a pool of blood, and Camille shuttered. She backed away from the offending view and bumped into the wall as though the contours of the room had changed without her senses registering the alterations. Time seemed to shift uncomfortably. It was an odd sensation, as though she had been here in this moment before, yet couldn't quite grasp the passage of the time. The familiarity was first, the utter disassociation came a fast second. Sweat stood out on Camille's brow, and she leaned against the cool wall for support. Whoever had lived here had left such a mark, a stain in the fabric of the space, that it would be difficult for anyone to settle here and not be haunted.

Camille edged into the dining area and stopped to look blindly

The Parrot Told Me

out the window. The familiarity of the scene steadied her. She and Monica had shared that at least. The tidy view of the vegetable garden, the rows of dried grey foliage clinging tenaciously to the soil, fenced in by neat white pickets. The huge lilac bush seemed to strain from its place next to the taller privacy fence, pushing limbs heavy with unopened blooms against the battered grey brown wood. Camille pressed chilled fingertips against the glass, heedless of the smeared ovals left on the windowpane.

She turned then, drawing a deep breath. The dining room was plainly a protest to convention. The sharp angles and searing colors seemed to challenge anyone who had the temerity to sit. A glass top table centered the space. Its sole occupant, a grotesque vase of putrid green, sprouted a boutique of dried and crumbling flower, their colors dulled into a universal parchment gold.

An easel had been set up opposite, leaving the artist full view of the room. The canvas was covered with a loose tarp.

Camille was suddenly anxious to see that painting, the last work of her ghostly neighbor. She bypassed the bookcase, empty of the intended contents and filled instead with a tottering stack of music CDs, to stand before the canvas. Her fingers hesitated as she felt the stiff fabric, but she was aware of the passing time. With a grand gesture, she tossed the cloth aside.

She wasn't sure if she cried out, but a high pitched sigh seemed to hang like a scent in the air. The painting was terrible. It was a visual sob. It was true. Talent warred with emotion in the work, and Camille felt a visceral response to it. She wanted to touch, yet she wanted to close her eyes. To feel, but escape.

A sound, like papers skittering against glass, made her look toward the window. The day was gray and she could see little through the fingerprinted glass. But when the sound came again, she drew up and shifted toward the window. Wings, light gray varying to the deepest charcoal, brushed against the glass.

Pigeons?

Footsteps in the hall without made her turn again. Ah, but she was she getting distracted. Her curiosity, usually voracious, had led her no further than the front room where she stood, slack jawed and gaping

With a shake, she trailed toward the kitchen. She feared that the decidedly odd Max might be pacing the hallway, waiting for her return. She had to find some remnant of the bird's as an excuse for her presence. Empty hands would make her seem little more than what she really was, a curious neighbor snooping.

The kitchen proved to be the mother load. In one corner, an obvious gap before the window revealed where the cage had once stood. There was even a scattering of seeds on the dusty linoleum. In a small cabinet to the right were all of the remaining bird supplies. With visibly trembling fingers, Camille laid out all of the toys and seed boxes, creating a great pile of excuses for her visit.

Rising to her knees, she glanced around for a bag to contain the things. She hated to spread her fingerprints throughout the small space, but she hadn't even considered wearing gloves. Grimacing with distaste, she pulled open cabinets covered in a film of dust and old grease, peered into dark shelves jumbled with exotic foods and old glassware, and scanned counter tops. By the phone there was a Tupperware full of pens and pencils and a tablet. Tacked on the wall above with scotch tape there was a list of numbers, heading them all was Mara Donahue. Her number had been scratched out with purple marker. No other number took its place, and Camille wondered briefly why Monica hadn't written a new number to replace the old. The remainder of the list consisted of pizza places, Chinese takeout, a doctor's office, and several names that had no labels. Some were merely initials.

Camille was so tempted to take it. In all of the movies, the intrepid female lead thought nothing of taking things from the scene of the crime. But Camille did not have that kind of confidence. There was a chance that Max had been here and had seen the list at one time. He might notice if it was missing. And he would definitely know who had taken it. Besides, time was running out, and she really needed to find that bag for the bird things.

"Could be in her bathroom," she murmured, her eyes going to the front door. She stood swiftly and headed down the hall, a mirror to her own. The master bedroom and bath were at the end of the hall, an office to the left and a second, smaller bath to the right.

She was intent on making it to the master bath to see the scene of what she believed was the murder, but the open door to the extra bedroom distracted her. Where her room was equipped with a second

The Parrot Told Me

hand computer desk, bookshelves, and chair; this room was very different. It held essentially no furniture. Instead, it boasted canvases. Stacked one against the other, five or six deep, lining every wall. Some were turned in to face the wall, while others were revealed in all their Technicolor glory. It was as breathtaking and terrible as before.

Camille could not turn away. She stepped cautiously within, but was soon flipping through canvases like an avid art collector.

Some were still lifes, their subjects depicted with hints of detail and bursts of color. Others were portraits, some nudes while others were almost formal with the subjects in elaborate dress. Still others were abstracts, made up totally of color and emotion.

The work in progress in this room was also covered, but this time a full palette lay next to the shrouded easel. Gooey globs of oil paints dotted the wax paper, smears of it blending into a rainbow of shades.

This was Monica's last work.

Camille didn't hesitate this time. She pulled the covering free and stepped back to view Monica's work.

"Last unfinished work," she murmured, studying the portrait. It was a man. Not too surprising there. There were at least a dozen other male models depicted on the other canvases. But this one was different. The detail was much more exacting, almost photo perfect. The subject was in action, almost as though he had been caught unaware, which lent a natural posture to his pose. He was seated on a bed, the blankets and sheets pooled around his hips leaving the long curve of his back naked to the striated pink-gold light slipping through the blinds of an unseen window. A second window cast a faded glow on the carpeted floor, the crystal clear glass revealing the familiar grays and greens of the back yard.

Camille could see every freckle on his back, every whisker bristling from his angled jaw, and each lash of his shuttered eyes. The man's position only revealed a sliver of his face. His salt and pepper hair gave Camille the impression that he was several years older than Monica. Then Monica had been, Camille mentally corrected herself.

Camille bent forward, her eyes caught by a strange mark on the man's shoulder. A tattoo. It appeared to be feline. A cat.

A breath of air snaked down Camille's neck and she shuttered. There was something not right about the portrait, although Camille could

30

not have said what.

A stutter of sound came from Camille's side and she spun around guiltily. Wings, as soft and undefined as before brushed the glass, making the hair stand on Camille's bare arms.

In a nervous gesture, Camille turned back toward the portrait, pulled the cloth from beneath the easel, and shook it out. She quickly jerked it up and over the canvas, feeling an almost instant relief when the man was no longer visible.

Camille quickly checked her watch and continued down the hall. She didn't want to be too late. She didn't want Max to become suspicious and come looking for her. Or worse yet, call Mrs. Patterson.

The master bedroom was incredible, red and plush and decadent. And familiar. It was obvious that this was where the portrait had been created, down to the last gilded tassels on the bed's canopy.

And that fact changed things. A naked man had recently been ensconced there, recently enough that the view out of the curtained window had barely changed seasons. And the intimacy was unmistakable. She shivered slightly, her mind insisting that she was on the verge of something. Something important.

Camille resisted the urge to touch the beaded throw draped over the foot of the bed and passed soundlessly into the bathroom. Master bath would have been a poor name for the tiny space. The apartment building had been constructed before the days of the spacious baths and whirlpool tubs. Instead, the snug room was outfitted with a toilet bedecked with a leopard topper, a pedestal sink, a small cabinet with glass doors revealing neatly stacked ruby towels, and a claw footed tub encased in a clear plastic curtain hanging from a circular rack. The curtain was pulled back and the tub was revealed in all its antique splendor. The scene was way too familiar for Camille's comfort. She had even purchased a similar cabinet from Target to store her own towels. The room called for some sort of storage, but still, the similarities were disconcerting.

Camille stepped in and slowly turned, eyes scanning plain white walls, the empty towel rack, and the half used box of tissues balanced precariously on the back of the toilet.

Her eyes were drawn irresistibly to the tub. On the window ledge above she could see the pale yellow and ruby candles, their wax pooled on the chipped wood of the sill. A thin line of hardened wax traced over

The Parrot Told Me

the ledge and froze in a perfect teardrop, almost like blood. Camille could recall Chloe's scandalized comment about the candles. A wry smile twisted her lips. Some scandal.

"The radio," Camille breathed, looking around for the weapon. But naturally it had been removed and all traces of the accident had been meticulously cleaned up. By who? Camille did wonder whose responsibility it was to fix the inevitable mess that Monica's death had created.

Camille studied the tub and the other objects in the room. If the radio had fallen in the tub, it must have been above the tub. Camille backed up to the doorway and leaned against the frame. There were only a few surfaces close to the tub that were large enough to hold a radio: the toilet back, the cabinet top, and the window ledge.

"The window's out," Camille murmured, absently biting a fingertip. There were too many candles lining the sill to allow for room of just one paperback, much less a radio.

The top of the toilet tank was possible. There was enough room. But a plug? Camille turned to study the leopard print. Camille was familiar with the bathroom's layout and as she suspected, the only plug was next to the sink, opposite the toilet. Not close enough unless Monica had used an extension cord to trace across the floor. Unlikely since Monica would have had to step over the cord when she climbed out of the tub.

So that left the cabinet. Conveniently close, right height.

But what did that really tell her? That the accident theory was plausible? That Monica, hands slick with scented bath bubbles, had reached up to turn the station and fumbled? It looked possible.

But something was wrong and Camille could feel it. What?

The bang on the door had her jumping, hand to heart. She slipped down the hall and into the living room as a muffled voice filtered through the panel.

"Camille?"

She was relieved that the voice was masculine and more curious than angry.

"Coming," she called out, rushing out of the bathroom and through the bedroom. She paused for a moment, swiping up a few of the bird supplies she had laid out in the kitchen.

She quickly unlocked the door and swung it open. Max was waiting. His hands were shoved in deep pockets and he was rocking back on his heels.

Camille stopped in the doorway, hovering awkwardly like a frustrated hostess.

"You done?" He didn't explain why he asked, but in her position, Camille couldn't object.

"Yeah," she said hastily. "I found the things I was looking for, but not a bag to put them in."

He moved back from the door and pulled one hand out of his pocket to push back a lock of hair. "I've got bags. I'll get one for you."

That said, he moved quickly back to his own apartment and disappeared. Moments later he returned with several small plastic bags. He seemed to be in a hurry, and Camille couldn't help but be influenced. She felt the urgency bleed over to her as she stuffed the bird food and toys into bags.

With a single glance back, Camille pulled the door closed under the watchful eye of the neighbor. His presence made her nervous; his intense gaze disconcerted her.

She pulled the keys from her pocket, bags and their contents spilling to the floor.

"Shoot," she muttered, pulling the offending key ring free and glaring at the mess.

Max dropped almost immediately and began scooping the things up for her. Camille bent to join him, carefully avoiding his gaze, uncomfortable with the proximity.

She didn't know why she had so lost her composure, but all she craved now was escape. She wouldn't have been more nervous had Monica's water logged corpse edged the door back open to watch the exchange.

"Got everything you need?"

"Yeah. Yes, thanks," she muttered, standing. 'Here's the key."

He silently took the ring and smiled slightly. "I'll be relieved to give this up," he said.

"Oh?" Camille took one cautious step back, glancing toward the stairs.

"It's getting creepy. It will be better when they clean the place

The Parrot Told Me

out; rent it again." He looked toward the closed door, his gaze dragging Camille's attention in the same direction.

"Sure, I can see that." Camille paused and looked from his still figure to the door as though some significant clue was pasted to the panel. Shaking herself, she straightened and shifted her bags. "Well, thanks."

"Sure," he responded and glanced down at the keychain. He paused for a second, looking for a moment as though he might say something more. She was subtly disappointed when he gave his head a little shake and eased into his apartment. Camille noticed that he bolted the door almost immediately.

So what was he afraid of?

Chapter 4

The blustery March morning was warming up nicely when Camille entered the bookstore. It was true that spring was finally thawing the brittle edges of winter and the signs could already be seen around campus. It seemed that even a breath of warmth had coeds dropping sweatshirts to tie around their waist, and jeans were shucked to reveal pale legs bristling with goose bumps.

Camille noticed little of these frivolities as she pulled her car into its habitual space and turned off the ignition. Belatedly, she noticed that her window had been left down and ignored it. She had the odd sensation that she just couldn't summon the energy to restart the car to fix the window.

It took an effort to get out of the car and close the door behind her. She paused for a moment, mentally shaking herself and physically straightening her shoulders, stretching her spine in a slow shrug.

She was moving briskly by the time she unlocked the door to the bookstore and pulled the heavy wooden door wide. There was some sort of satisfaction in the view. The once failing grand building had been renovated for its new inhabitants, its style retelling stories about the people it had once housed. She and Leo had painstakingly picked through fabrics and wall coverings in an attempt to pick period pieces. The bookcases were incredible in themselves. Leo's brother specialized in architectural salvage, and he had found treasures from scores of local and distant homes. The crown molding, shelving, and furniture were all dating from the late 1800's and early 1900's.

Just the space gave Camille the confidence that she needed. She had a mission, and she wouldn't be dissuaded from it that easily.

Locking the door behind her, she hurried to the desk and dropped her coat and purse on the counter. Quickly, she booted up the computer and eased up on her stool.

She had a name, now she needed more. Max's accidental name

The Parrot Told Me

dropping had yielded Camille's first real clue. Max himself may or may not have been involved with Monica, but her best friend shouldn't have such qualms about revealing information as a past lover might.

The second clue had come in the form of the woman's last name as it was noted on the list within the apartment. Mara Donahue. Max's guess at the name had been close. Now all she had to do was find her. The phone book had given a number, and Camille had spent her first minutes at work looking up the address in the computer. Her Google map program gave her an exact location, a quick twenty minute drive from Camille's own apartment.

She glanced furtively over her shoulder. If Leo caught her at this, it would be another long speech about how Camille was using this whole made up mystery to fill up her own sadly empty existence. Perhaps his wording would be kinder, but the content would be the same. Besides, she hadn't decided if she would even admit to her exploration of the dead woman's apartment. She was a terrible liar, and chances were, if Leo asked, she would spill every last lurid detail. It was much easier to just ignore the subject.

A rush of air raised goose bumps and pulled Camille's attention from the computer. Leo. In full leather from the precisely tailored jacket, slick black pants, and loafers, he cut an impressive figure. Even his socks were a matching black. Camille supposed he had simply been unable to find leather ones.

She quickly printed out the area map and closed down the program. As the printer hummed, she turned away from the screen to face her friend.

"Morning, doll," he greeted, his face alight with a general self-satisfied smile. He must have had a good evening. He looked brilliant, a male glow.

"Morning," Camille responded cautiously, her eyes following his lithe figure as he circled around the counter. "You look awfully," she paused, scanning his features, "smug."

"I had a good night's rest," he said, dropping a casual arm around her shoulders. "Wish I could say the same for you."

"What do you mean?" she asked, pulling away. She had thought that her sleepless night had been cleverly disguised by a little makeup. Murder mysteries and neurotic birds did not make good bedfellows.

Rachael Rawlings

"You look tired. I know that you'd prefer I not notice." He raised a conciliatory hand. "Don't get mad. Just give me a chance."

"I'm not mad," Camille responded, a trifle wearily. "You're right. I didn't sleep well." When he looked like he'd comment, she tipped her face up to look in his eyes. "Just don't ask right now."

"That's almost irresistible," he said, his expression difficult to read. He studied her, his playful mood melting like a Popsicle dropped on hot pavement. "I'll control myself."

Camille smiled back, grateful.

Leo sighed and moved closer to her. He was the kind of man who could do that. Apply just the right pressure at the back of her neck with just the right expression of concern. "You going to see Mom this evening?"

Camille ran her fingers through her cropped locks and pulled away. "I'm just going to get through the day. I don't have any plans past that."

"And that is all you need?"

The subtle question was there. He was waiting for her to spill her guts as she usually did. He wanted her to rage. To throw a girl fit, fuss and fume about whatever it was that preyed on her mind. The honesty and impulsivity that normally impressed him, that made her so familiar to him, was stifled for once in a long while. Camille turned around and nodded silently.

God, she wanted to tell. She ached to tell. He was her best friend. He sat with her when she got her ears pierced, all three times. He brought her take out during the flu season. He came to visit her family at Christmas and baked cookies with her mom.

But he was also a self-proclaimed protector who had seen her at her most desperate. He had been the big brother during the rocky early college years, the emergency date for dorm dances, the crazy companion for Halloween high jinx, and the shoulder to cry on when the world just got too big.

But he hadn't been there that one night. That one night that had changed her life.

Camille blinked hard to clear her eyes of the threat of tears and the blur of memories. Perhaps she did just need her mother.

"Leo, you're a sweetheart. But yes, I probably do need to stop by

37

The Parrot Told Me

home." She noted the hope fill his eyes and hated her next words. "I think I need to do this one alone."

The veneer of sophisticated disinterest that he rarely used with her slipped into place and Camille felt a second stab of guilt. "We'll go together soon," she said brightly, trying to look casual, as though she didn't see that she had hurt him.

"Sure. Whenever," he returned, and looked away.

Camille heaved a sigh and pulled her purse and coat off of the counter top. "If you're ready, we can open up. I just have to put my things away."

He nodded his assent and headed toward the door. With his back turned, she snatched the printed map from the machine and stuffed it in her purse. She glanced back once and headed back towards the office, holding tight to her secrets.

~*~

Mara's home was in one of those neighborhoods where each home reflects the others to such a degree that only the color of the front door and the distinctive car in the driveway identified where you belonged. Mara had done little to set her house apart from the others. The flowerbeds were still bare, with no bushes or ornamental trees to fill the space.

Her front door was a basic brown, her shutters a matching shade. Her address was drawn in simple numbers to the left of the door. There was no car is her driveway, and no garage for her to park in. It didn't look like anyone was home.

Feeling like a stalker, Camille parked outside the house and peered through the car window. It surprised her a little to see that Monica had a friend settled so peacefully in suburbia. So much for knowing her neighbor. She checked her watch. She had already been sitting here for fifteen minutes. Something told her that behind one of those sets of curtains in a neighboring house there was a concerned busybody just waiting to call the cops.

Camille sighed. This discussion would have to wait. She continued a few blocks up and turned around in a handy driveway. After a moment, she pulled off in front of an empty lot, slid out of the driver's

38

seat, and closed her car door. With her lip caught in her teeth, she pulled her jacket closer around her hunched shoulders and walked briskly along the side of the road. It took her only a few minutes to reach Mara's house, but this time, instead of passing it, she went determinedly up the walk to the tidy front porch. Glancing over her shoulder, she made a show of knocking on the door, even though she was sure that no one was home. Leaning in closer, she could see the dim interior of the front room.

The furnishings were much more interesting than the exterior would have led her to believe. There was a velvet covered settee with an elegant curved back and clawed feet sitting cozily next to a wooden table graced with an antique stained glass tiffany type lamp. Her view was limited, but she could still see the pattern of the oriental carpet that covered hardwood floors, and the corner of a fireplace with white painted mantel.

On the wall facing the door, hung above the settee, was a painting. It drew Camille's attention almost immediately. With its strokes of color, it was distinctly contemporary in an otherwise traditional room. But its style was also familiar, and Camille would have bet money that the work was Monica's. Interesting.

The sound of a car passing made Camille pull away from the door and take a step back. With a nervous look, she pushed her hair back from her forehead and tugged her collar up closer to her throat.

"Time to go," she muttered, and hurried back to her car.

~*~

Camille opened the unlocked door without hesitation, pulling it closed after her to block her mother's dog, Bart, from fleeing into the yard beyond. Bart was an elderly hound who lived with the misguided notion that there was always something very exciting and very desirable lying just outside the confines of his own space. His running had been restricted in the last several years by his age and achy hips. Unfortunately, age has also reduced his eyesight significantly, but his hound dog nose would never fail him.

Camille bent and smoothed her hands down his slick coat, giving an extra stroke to his velvety ears. He panted his pleasure and followed her when she rose and traced her way to the living room. There she

The Parrot Told Me

slipped out of her coat and dropped it along with her purse on the nearest chair as she followed the scent of fresh coffee into the deeper recesses of the house.

It was typical of her mother to have coffee on, and almost as much for fresh muffins or other bakery goods to be artfully arranged on the counter. While the treats weren't always homemade, they were always delicious. It was one of her mother's homey touches that Camille liked best.

"Hey," Camille said, dropping into the chair opposite her mother.

"There you are," her mother exclaimed, a smile lighting her deep hazel eyes.

"Thought I'd just stop by," Camille said, easing back in her chair. "Any coffee left? It smells great."

"Plenty," her mother replied and rose to pour a cup.

"You don't have to wait on me, Mom," Camille scolded, but didn't rise. She watched in amusement as her mother added the precise amount of sugar and cream that Camille liked. "So where's dad?"

"In the garden, like usual."

"Um, what is growing now?"

Camille's mother chuckled. "I doubt anything, but he's preparing for the spring."

"Always," Camille agreed.

"And how's our bookstore?" Camille's mother asked, sipping from her own cup.

Camille relaxed and spent the soft evening hours as the sun retired behind the lacy twining of the trees, talking about her work, the ins and outs of the business that her mother had encouraged her to pursue. She added comments about Leo, knowing that her mother wanted to hear about him as well. She knew that her mother sheltered a very soft place in her heart for the motherless friend that Camille had adopted during her high school years.

As the evening waned, Camille became acutely aware that she was holding out on her mother. It was rare for her to hold her tongue on anything, but she knew that her experience with Monica was off limits. She was close to her parents, but there was something else there. There was always something else, undefined and better left that way, a reticence that Camille could never overcome. Camille's eyes unwillingly

40

strayed to the mantle where the history of her family was spelled out in blurred black and whites, yellowed glossies, and the precise Technicolor photographs of present day. There were some missing. The tacky photo of she and her sister in homemade bikinis with protruding toddler bellies was gone. And the high school snap shot of her sister and her friends, arms around each other and hats askew.

Camille stood before she was aware of the urge. She went slowly, her stride slow and careful. She suddenly understood what it meant to be walking on egg shells, and wondered how long she had subconsciously been doing just that.

"Where's Darcy's picture?"

Camille's mother looked momentarily stunned and Camille felt her face flush. How long had it been since that name had passed her lips in her mother's presence?

"What do you mean?" Carol's voice sounded genuinely baffled.

"The pictures? The photos?" Camille heard the sharp tone creep into her voice and hated it. Didn't want it, but couldn't seem to avoid it. In her mind, a desperate childish voice was shouting, shut up!

Carol stood and smoothed her slacks, her hands suddenly nervous. "Camille, I just moved some things around."

"But Darcy's pictures?" Camille snapped. The little voice moaned.

Her mother still had that look on her face, like she had just been struck. Camille ran a hand through her cropped hair in frustration, guilt sliding through her veins like a fast moving virus. Slowly she sat back down, deliberately resting her open hands, palms up, in her lap. She ordered her limbs to stop shaking and froze there for a moment, letting the emotion drain.

With regret she met her mother's eyes. "I'm sorry," she murmured softly, feeling the ache rise in her throat.

Her mother rose, running her fingertips over her forehead. She sighed softly and bent her head, suddenly much older than her 56 years.

"You know I haven't forgotten, Cam," she said, her tone slightly cool.

"I know, I know," Camille said, dropping her eyes to her open hands. "It's just, when I didn't see the picture..."

"You thought I forgot? You thought, just like that, that I forgot?

The Parrot Told Me

Or that I'm trying to forget? That I could?"

"No, mom," Camille gasped. "No, I never."

They stood for a long moment, words hanging thick as smoke between them, years of unspoken utterances.

With a gesture, Carol turned and looked toward the mantle. "I'll fix it later."

"Mom, I'm sorry," Camille repeated, her fingers brushing her mother's sleeve.

Carol caught her hand, gave a gentle squeeze, and released her. It was a gesture of forgiveness and comfort. But Camille knew that she had hurt her mother and felt a slow sting for what she had caused.

Chapter 5

That evening, Camille curled up in silence in the warmth of her bedroom and propped a notebook in her lap. Written in her familiar scrawl was the word for word dictation from Camille's new pet.

At a distance, it looked insane. Who would ever believe that someone could take this seriously? How had she jumped from the squawked monologue of a nervous bird to the belief that its owner was murdered?

The written words refused to tell. And Camille was feeling the common sensation of her world tipping out of control. What would her therapist say? Get out? Let go? Post limitations? She hadn't seen her therapist since early college days and it was beginning to look like she needed a new one.

"Drat and double drat!" she growled, and looked back to her list.

Camille uncapped the pen and absently chewed on the top. It was time to build a plan. She would go only so far and then give up on this rather macabre chase. She would talk to Monica's best friend. Yes, that was good. If nothing else, they could talk about Monica's painting, since it was obvious that Mara was both familiar with and appreciated it. And maybe she could check about the man in the painting. The man that Monica had obviously been involved with. But no further. If Mara, Monica's best friend, was comfortable with the untimely death, Camille would be as well.

Camille noted her intentions and wrote a brief list of questions to as Mara. That is, if Mara agreed to be honest with Camille. When Camille had called her earlier in the evening, Mara had sounded fully prepared to tell Camille where to go, and it wasn't a pleasant suggestion. And that was without knowing Camille had been parked outside her house. But after some consideration, Mara had agreed upon a meeting, one in which she could control the rules. She chose where, when, and for how long. And there she left it, with the unspoken promise of information pending. And if there wasn't? Camille plucked the pen cap

The Parrot Told Me

from between her teeth and snapped it in place. She wouldn't consider a glitch in her plan. She was on track, had a goal, and was set in her course.

Sleep came with satisfactory ease.

~*~

Mara's reluctance to meet, while evident over the phone, was even more so in person. Her very stance, chubby hands planted firmly on abundant hips, implied that she was not a woman to be bullied.

Camille couldn't help but be startled when the other woman beckoned her from the bar. Camille had just assumed that Monica's best friend would somehow be a reflection of Monica herself, similar in dress, style, and appearance.

Camille tried hard not to stare at the too tight pants, raw silk at a guess, stretched across the flat expanse of the other woman's rear, bounding and scrunching as she strolled with confidence between tightly configured tables and chairs. Camille followed in her wake, the patrons parting like gaping guppies as Mara brushed by, imperial in her girth.

At the table, Mara put in her order with the preciseness of a school teacher instructing English, adding in an astounding number of withs and withouts to boggle the mind of even the most experienced waiter.

When the young man taking the order left, his eyebrows hanging somewhere around his bleached bangs, Mara placed her elbows on the table and folded her be ringed hands primly in her lap.

"I doubt I have anything to tell you that you don't already know, she said flatly, her voice unengaging.

"I'm honestly not sure myself," Camille admitted. "As I told you, I ended up with Simon..."

"Good thing too," Mara snapped. "I wouldn't have put up with that squawking, shit making beast for a day."

Momentarily shocking into silence, Camille forced herself to close her gaping mouth and paste a half smile on her face.

"Yes, well, I like birds," she said, picking up her water glass and taking a quick sip. With an audible swallow, she looked back into Mara's still sour visage. "But I was surprised when Monica left Simon to me. I mean, I really didn't know her very well."

"Don't feel bad. Not many people knew Monica very well. She liked it like that." Mara glanced up from her wine list and signaled with one vague gesture to the waiter.

"But you did."

Mara sighed and rested her rounded elbows on the pristine white tablecloth. "She was my friend, yes, but there were things that I didn't know about. I told you over the phone."

"I know, and I appreciate that you agreed to meet me." Camille found herself rushing her words, as though the woman might get up and leave unexpectedly, suddenly. "I just noticed that Simon seems to be having problems adjusting and I wondered what he was missing. I don't really know much about his life before."

Mara was frowning, and Camille felt the heat creep into her face. She felt like the other woman was reading her easily, and didn't like what she was seeing.

"Bullshit," Mara said, pausing when the waiter stopped by to deliver the drinks. When he backed away, Mara resumed as though she hadn't been disturbed in the slightest. "That isn't close to what you want to know. You want to know about Monica. Now what I want to know is why."

Camille weighed the other woman wearily. She had avoided even admitting her suspicions to her best friend or to her family. How safe was this person?

"I think your friend was murdered."

If she had expected some great reaction, she plainly wasn't going to get it. Mara's eyes pinned her like a helpless insect before the windshield hit. She just prayed that the other woman would blink soon and break that silver blue gaze.

The waiter chose that moment to arrive and start divvying out plates, shuffling through the complex sides and add-ons with a nervous laugh. He left without asking if everything suited their needs, doubtless praying that he had washed his hands of them. Camille could sympathize. She wished that she didn't have to stay under Mara's glare.

The silence was painful. Camille sampled the meal with little enthusiasm, although the food may have been the best she had ever eaten for quite a while. It was certainly priced high enough to warrant a double take at the bill and Camille knew that the bill would be hers when they

The Parrot Told Me

left, so she was really hoping for a better response than Mara's total absorption in her meal.

Mara ate with the single minded shoveling of a person who wanted to waste no time during the meal. She wanted to get away. That much was evident.

"Well?" Camille's tone was uncomfortably strident in her ears.

"Well?" Mara glanced up and picked up her glass. "You want me to comment? Fine. You're crazy. It was an accident." Mara's smooth tones sunk into a hiss and she leaned forward, her hefty bosom almost dipping into her gravy splotched plate. "I won't be involved in this, and I have two really good reasons. One," she said, holding up a chubby finger boasting a slender silver band, "you are dead wrong and it was an accident, and two, if you were right, the folks who are responsible would take you out like old garbage."

It was the closest thing to a threat that Camille had received and she had a difficult time controlling her breathing.

"But I..."

"Shut up," Mara interrupted, still leaning in close. "You have no idea what you're talking about and what you're sticking your nose into. I do. My best advice is to shoot the damn bird and get on with your life. Monica was way over your head in too many ways."

The waiter chose that unfortunate time to stop back by, and Mara retreated back into her seat. The look Mara pinned him with would turn anyone a trifle green, and he was no exception. He waited in silence, as though worried that a single utterance might bring on a fierce tirade from the scowling Mara. Mara impatiently waved him away, and he turned smartly and moved away at a fast pace, dodging skillfully around occupied tables and other waiters.

"So you won't help," Camille said softly after the waiter disappeared into the kitchen.

"I gave you my advice," Mara replied. "There is nothing else I can do for you. I just hope you don't pursue this."

"But she was your friend," Camille protested.

"And a big girl who knew what she was doing," Mara replied flatly, dropping her cloth napkin on her plate in one frustrated gesture and rising.

Camille felt a sense of helplessness but could do nothing to stop the other woman. She watched as Mara sailed through the restaurant, casting barely a glance to her right and left as she went.

Camille almost cried when she got the bill.

~*~

The ride home was lengthy, and Camille was in no mood for petty nuisances. A pesky March snow was more of an annoyance than a true threat, but the fat flakes that spattered her windshield also obscured her view and smeared in wet streaks across the glass. It was a bad time to realize she needed new wipers.

In frustration, she gripped the wheel and leaned forward to peer out into the messy darkness. Drat but this whole thing was frustrating. She had had no idea what she was getting into when she had sought out Mara, and now she almost regretted the move. It wasn't that she felt her ideas were without merit. If anything, Mara had reinforced them. Whoever or whatever Monica had been involved in was dubious enough to make her friend think it might be worth killing for.

Camille eased her foot off the gas and noted cars around her slowing down as well. She carefully tapped her brake and frowned. Her mind was still spinning and she once again tried to picture Monica's apartment. She had missed something, she was sure.

Traffic was crawling by the time she gratefully turned off New Circle and headed into town. The ramps were slick with the wet snow, but still maneuverable. She debated for a moment, trying to decide what to do about Leo. Should she tell him about this conversation? With a sigh, she steered her car away from her own apartment and headed in town toward his. Perhaps it was time to fess up.

~*~

Leo's controlled features barely registered his surprise at their unexpected arrival on his doorstep. Snowflakes frosted her hair and shoulders, melting into glassy beads as Leo backed away from the door and gestured her into the heat.

"Snow getting bad?" he asked, stepping forward to close the door.

The Parrot Told Me

"Not too much yet, but it still might be ugly come morning," she responded, dropping her coat on one of his kitchen chairs.

"And you were out because?"

Camille sighed and shook the moisture from her cropped hair. "Give me a glass of wine? I have a confession to make and the Catholic in me likes ceremony."

Leo waved her to a seat and disappeared into the kitchen. Moments later he returned with two brimming wineglasses and an unopened bottle tucked under his arm.

"Just in case," he said and dropped on the couch opposite.

Camille gratefully took her glass and sipped, letting the smooth fruity taste fill her mouth and ease, like warm honey, down her throat.

"Okay, so spill it." Leo sat back, hands folded in the perfect picture of patience.

"You're going to lecture, but try to go easy."

He waved his hand carelessly, a gesture to erase the words.

"I went to meet Monica's friend, Mara."

"Monica, as in, dead lady?"

"Yep. I got Mara's name from Monica's neighbor and called."

Leo took a long swallow of wine and set his glass carefully on the glossy black tabletop.

"You asked Monica's neighbor for the name of her friend?"

"Not exactly. I asked the neighbor about the bird and if he could let me grab some supplies from Monica's apartment."

"Damn, Camille!"

Camille ducked her head and cupped her glass close to her chest. She ran cold fingertips around the rim of her glass. The liquid shuttered. She realized she was trembling slightly.

"I knew you wouldn't approve, which is why didn't say anything. But I did get some information. Max told me he didn't know anything about the bird, but that Mara might."

"Max is the neighbor?"

"Yes," Camille said, wisely refraining from mentioning about how strange she thought the elusive Max might be. But she felt a flutter of relief when she recognized the emergence of curiosity in Leo's tone.

"And he volunteered all of this help?"

"I was bugging him a little. He has a key to the apartment, and, well, caved."

"So you went in there?"

"I needed to get some things for Simon. He's been so depressed," she let her voice trail off on this half-truth and avoided his perceptive gaze. He would see too much. He always saw too much.

"Bull," Leo said succinctly.

"Well, part of it was true. The bird was depressed."

"And you were so curious that you had to see the scene of the crime. Go ahead. Deny it. You were all over the apartment, sticking your nose into her private stuff."

"Hey," Camille protested loudly. "Back off! Even you must admit that things look fishy; I had a reason."

Leo heaved a sigh and leaned his head back. Camille watched, interested, as he mentally counted backwards, gradually diffusing his temper. When he looked back at her, his eyes had calmed.

"Okay, so you got the neighbor to hand over the keys, and then what?"

"I went in," Camille said, a faintly victorious thrill tracing down her spine. She had him. He was interested. "I did get to see most of the place." She briefly described the apartment as she had found it, detailing the phone list and the bathroom. "I took the number and called Monica's friend, just to get her impression of how Monica lived." When Leo would have spoken, she raised a silencing hand. "I know that I said it was the bird, and it is. But as much as it might be an accident, Simon's story and the paintings in the apartment were just plain spooky. I know that it isn't much proof of anything, but Mara's attitude today certainly seemed a little off."

"And what did she have to say?" Leo's tone was just this side of patronizing, but Camille ignored it.

"She as much as admitted that Monica was involved in something illegal. She was trying to warn me off!"

"And you won't listen."

"No." Camille paused. "Well, yes, I listened. I don't want to get mixed up in anything dangerous, but I'm not going to let this just lie either."

"Ridiculous, Camille, why? Why can't you just call the cops, report what you think, and leave it alone?"

The Parrot Told Me

Camille sat back and put her hand over her eyes. "I just can't, Leo."

Behind the darkness, she could feel his frustration surge and recede. "Okay, fine. But we do this together. NO more sneaking into apartments. No more solo investigations. Anything you do, you do with me."

Camille grinned, "Agreed, partner."

~*~

When Camille heard knocking early the next morning, she automatically swung open the door, expecting Leo. No one came to visit her on Sunday mornings. But she was wrong on this count. Max had come to call.

Camille was momentarily speechless, painfully aware of her tattered sweatshirt, gym shorts, and huge stuffed moose slippers with their wide eyes staring up at the ceiling.

Max, in contrast, had improved considerably. His hair was still long, pulled back in a neat ponytail at the nape of his neck, but the beard was trimmed down to a nubby shadow and contacts had replaced the thick lenses glasses.

"Hi," he said, his eyes tracing a deliberate line from her tousled hair to her slippered feet. "Should I come back at a better time?"

Camille flushed at the implication and back away from the door. "No, of course not. Now is fine." She shyly gestured him through the door, a high school awkwardness momentarily descending.

"Good. I have to go in to work this evening, so I wanted to catch you before you headed out." He shuffled slightly, a grimace on his face. "I've not been particularly cooperative with you, and I thought I'd drop by to check on the, you know, bird."

"You're concerned about the bird?"

"Not exactly." He glanced down the hall, looking uncomfortably like someone with a secret. "Can I sit down for a sec?"

Camille felt a moment of unease but couldn't really credit it. He had shown no signs of suspicious behavior. Not really. "Sure," she said forcing a smile.

They moved into the living room, and Camille gestured him onto

50

the couch while she took the chair. Automatically, she toed off her bulky slippers and tucked her bare feet beneath her.

"I've heard some new things about Monica," Max said shortly, his eyes not an intent blue gaze. "And I know you've been asking questions; you need to stop."

"What?" Camille heard her voice rise.

"I've heard, well, I know that you went through the apartment. And I know that you talked to Mara, pissed her off royally. So she calls me and rips me a new one."

"That doesn't surprise me a bit," Camille said flatly. "And I did talk to Mara. My God, something is wrong here and no one gives a damn!"

"Wrong? Yeah, Monica is dead, but the cops call it an accident or something like that. They're done with it, why aren't you?"

"Because now, suddenly, everyone is worried about my questions and what started as just an idea is seeming more and more real."

Max sighed and pinched the bridge of his nose, like someone accustomed to glasses.

"I think you're wrong about Monica. I really do." Max pinned her with the look again. "But if you're not, if you're right, could chasing after a killer be a good thing?"

Camille looked at him in frustrated silence.

"Tell the cops; give this up."

Camille sighed. "I have certainly heard that before," she mumbled.

"Will you?"

"I'm not sure." She ran her had through her cropped hair. "I just couldn't read Mara. I couldn't tell where she was coming from." She gave him a sidelong gaze. "And I wouldn't have expected her to be involved with you."

"Me?" He sounded incredulous. "I barely know her, but she sure as hell knows everyone and everything about Monica."

"An odd pair," Camille murmured.

"Yeah," Max said, "but they've worked together forever."

"Where?"

"Nelson and Tower," Max replied, distracted. His eyes scanned

51

The Parrot Told Me

the living room and came to rest on Camille's face. "Look, you seem to be a nice person. Maybe you're a little too curious, but I think you mean well."

Camille nodded slowly. "I do mean well."

Max rose and headed toward the door. "Then take care of yourself and avoid all of this. Don't get in any more trouble than necessary."

Camille found herself agreeing as she eased the door closed, the lie sour on her tongue. But at least she had something new. Nelson and Tower.

Chapter 6

She had hoped that Leo wouldn't be there when she got to work. Sundays were usually slow, and they opened at noon, still an hour away. She could have used a few minutes of quiet time, just to think, to mull over all of her quandaries. But she knew her chances weren't great. It was a rarity, but she had been known to beat him if she was driven by a caffeine overload. But all the coffee in the world wouldn't help her today. Leo was in full big brother mode, and it was written all over his handsome face.

"Hey," he greeted, standing over a carton of newly printed books, the scent of fresh paper and ink slightly intoxicating.

"Hey yourself," she responded, walking deftly by to slip into the office. The smell of coffee overrode the particular bookstore air and made Camille think of her mother's home. With a sigh, she dropped her purse and hung her jacket on the hall tree next to Leo's leather coat.

She rifled through some mail and poured herself a cup of coffee. She was anxious to tell Leo about Max's visit, but had mixed feelings about Max himself. Did she trust him? Should she? Having an ally within the building would be a huge advantage. Befriending a murderer would not.

With coffee in hand, she went up to the main desk and eased up on her stool, watching with silent interest as Leo worked. His attempt at silence did not last long.

"Anything new going on?" he asked, hitching a hip on one of their padded stools. She frowned at him, half enjoying the way even taking a seat could be performed with such masculine grace. Not a hair out of place and a perfect chiseled profile. She felt positively dumpy next to him and wished, too late, that she had used some of that under eye cream this morning to get rid of the puffiness.

"Not really," she said, carefully placing her coffee on the counter and taking her own stool. "Busy this morning?"

The Parrot Told Me

"I'll open in a minute," he responded, eyeing her with some suspicion. "So why so prickly?"

"I had a visitor," Camille explained, and described her conversation with Max. She had wanted those few extra minutes to edit her story, but didn't have that chance. Instead, she told him all and hoped that his deeply ingrained masculinity wouldn't make him distrust the word of her neighbor.

She could see her luck wasn't holding. Leo's pleasant expression firmed into a stern frown and he crossed his muscular arms over his equally well defined chest in a tight X.

"Doesn't sound good," he said. "I want to meet this guy."

"You want to meet Max?" She said, her voice rising innocently. "Why?"

"Why do you think? I want to find out for myself what you're getting into."

"I'm not a child," Camille said tartly, unconsciously twirling an earring in her fingers.

"But you're not giving up, either."

"Well, no," she snapped. "And you're making me regret I ever said anything."

"Why?" He set out a slow exhalation of air. "I know you don't want to give up, but you're being typically reckless. You probably opened the door for this guy with no questions."

"I had questions, and yes, I was careful. Give me a little credit."

"And if he was going to hurt you? Did you have a plan?"

"Really, Leo, you're getting carried away!"

"Am I? You're the one insisting there was a murder. It's your bird who's the witness."

"I know," she said abruptly. She glanced at the floor, fuming silently.

"Did you ever think any of this has to do with Darcy?"

Her head jerked up, her chin raising several notches. "What do you mean? How could my sister have anything to do with this?"

"I'm not saying she does, but you have to admit, it's colored the way you behave sometimes."

"Maybe so," she said tightly. Her hands dropped to her lap and she found herself picking at her fingernails unconsciously. "God, you sound like my mom sometimes."

Leo almost smiled. "I'll take that as a compliment in this situation. And you never did tell me, how was the visit home?"

"It was fine," she said slowly, running her fingers through her hair, avoiding his eyes.

"And that's a lie," Leo said softly, kindly. His eyes flitted form her face back to the closed door. It was time to open, but she could see that he wouldn't budge.

"What do you mean?" Her tone was too sharp and she knew it.

"You have that look. Come on, give me some credit for experience, at least. You didn't look this bad when you made your grand confession the other night."

"It was awful," she admitted and eased off her stool to lean against the counter. With a pained expression, she recounted her discussion with her mother about the photograph of Darcy. "I don't know why I got so touchy. And before you say it, I know it has nothing to do with Monica." She reached up to twirl an earring, her lips tight. "I know she's really hurt by what I said, but I can't do anything to help. I seem to do this all the time; I just talk without thinking."

"That happens to everyone, Camille," Leo responded. "And this was your mother. She'd forgive anything you did, and you know that too."

"Maybe that's what makes it so hard. She does forgive anything, and God knows I've disappointed her plenty. But to involve Darcy was just one step too far. A step I never should have taken."

"Darcy was your sister. You have reason to grieve."

"But she was Mom's daughter. Her first. I think her reasons trump mine."

"This isn't a game," Leo argued, looking at Camille with concern. "I know her disappearance must be torture for your parents, but you lived through it too."

"I survived it," Camille breathed, wishing for the millionth time that she had known Leo then, when she was so alone.

Leo pulled his stool close and looked intently at Camille. "I know that it's a painful subject, but why don't you talk to your mom about Darcy?"

"I do," Camille insisted, frowning.

The Parrot Told Me

"No, Camille, you don't. You don't discuss it with anyone. I've known you for years and you've never even told me the whole story."

Camille raised her eyes in surprise, a little hurt showing in her pale face. To her, the story seemed so close, so much a part of her that she couldn't imagine that she hadn't discussed it. But perhaps he was right. She had spent so much time getting through it, she had never shared it, not even with her best friend, or worse yet, her mother.

"Oh, Leo, it was such a long time ago. I just..." She caught her lip in her teeth.

"I'm not looking for entertainment."

She sighed and pressed her hand against the counter. "Sometimes I hate to stir it all up." At the expression on his face, she ducked her head. "We were just a normal family. Darcy was older, so I irritated the crap out of her, and we argued a lot. But then we made up. She would hang out with me on weekends, or when her friends weren't available. She was really enjoying preparing me for high school. She liked being the mentor, and honestly, she was pretty good at it."

"She the brain in the family?"

"Well, yeah, pretty much." Camille closed her eyes, trying to sketch in the details of the face that had become much too vague. "Darcy was always the good student. She worked hard at her grades, but a lot of it just came naturally. And she held down a job after school at the ice cream place." Camille stood and began to pace even as the sweet flavor of borrowed treats brought up equally sweet memories. "It was late summer. Oh, sometimes it feels like yesterday. Darcy and I had been talking that night in my room. She had just broken up with her most current boyfriend and wanted a sounding board. It wasn't that she really cared that much about him," Camille slowly ran her hands through her hair, "she just wanted to talk." She could picture her sister, informally attired in a loose UK tee shirt and cut off sweat pants, her gaze intense and somehow confused with a tangle of teenage emotions. "She told me about all of his bad habits and the stuff that she thought was disgusting about guys in general," here Camille smiled at the memory of girl talk shared in the deepening gloom of a summer night. "And she went back to her room at about ten or so. Sometime after that she went out for a walk. She didn't tell us that part, the police did." Camille's voice sagged under the weight of the emotions. She could almost smell the heavy lilac

56

scent on the air seeping through the cracked window. The July heat had been fierce, the humidity worse.

"And the next morning, she was still gone."

The heat is what had hit her first. Her room was so warm, too warm for all the air being blown around by the ancient fan. Her window was open.

"I went to close the window and then stopped. I don't know why. But I knew something was wrong. I went to my door and opened it, really slowly. The house was quiet. I went to my parent's room across the hall first, but they were still asleep. I went to Darcy's next."

No words could describe it. The room had been barely disturbed. But it was all so frighteningly wrong.

"After I called my parents, I sat outside in the hallway, shaking. I knew that she was gone. I knew that something awful had happened, and nothing would ever be the same."

Leo stayed where he was, his long legs stretched to allow booted feet to shuffle uncomfortably on the floor. "And the police never found anything?"

"No. The neighbor said they thought they had seen her out walking. They weren't sure. And by the time we tried to retrace her steps, she was just gone."

~*~

That evening Camille got very drunk. It was the most she had imbibed in for years, but she wanted nothing but to forget. Darcy's lovely face swam in and out of her consciousness like Marley's ghost, tangible yet fleeting, dragging behind her the links of Camille's guilt like a chain.

Morning dawned hard and brittle, the temperature fluctuating like a nervous bride. The sun seemed to hang in the sky, deliberately assaulting Camille's tender senses. With trembling hands, Camille pulled the heavy drapes over her living room windows and made her way to the kitchen. She wasn't a habitual drunk, but she knew that coffee tended to be the standard remedy.

As the coffee-maker burped and spluttered, she forced herself to dress in loose jeans and a plain white tee shirt. When she returned to the living room, she was greeted with the welcome scent of coffee and a

The Parrot Told Me

slightly clearer head.

A knock at her door stopped her in her tracks. On bare feet, she padded to the door and peered through the peephole. Leo. Well, it was better than her curious neighbors, Chloe being the worst, Max running a recent close second.

"Let me in," Leo softly chanted, his face close to door. Camille watched him cast a cautious glance down the hall. "Get me out of here before your neighbor catches me," he hissed.

Camille smiled despite her aching head. She waited an extra minute, just to make him sweat. After his third knock, she opened the door and stepped aside as he slid in.

"Avoiding someone?" Camille asked sweetly.

"Your friendly neighborhood vamp got a hold of my number and has called me three times already," he said, locking the door behind him. "I don't know how she got it, but if I find out it was you, I'm posting yours in the restroom at the gas station."

"It wasn't," Camille replied archly, trying to suppress the smile. "But you're in the book, and Chloe isn't stupid. Just because her breasts are the size of melons doesn't mean she's illiterate."

Leo looked as though he doubted that statement, but said nothing. He moved in utter comfort from Camille's living room and into the compact kitchen. Simon watched in suspicious silence, pacing slowly up and down his perch, his head cocked.

"Nice look," Leo stated, gesturing to the closed drapes. "Early funeral home or late cave?"

"Unfortunate hangover," she responded, her voice deliberately light.

"Hung-over? You?" Concern bloomed on his expressive face, making him look older. "I'm just assuming it wasn't a party."

"I wanted to relax."

"Drown your sorrows, more like."

"That too." Camille turned away from his too intent eyes and busied herself by pouring him a cup of coffee.

"Want to talk about it?"

Camille shook her head, then winced at the pain.

"You okay then?"

"Fine," Camille said, flashing him a half smile. "Just dandy.

From my toes up, I feel like crap, but below that, I'm in great shape." She made a face at his smile and turned back to the counter.

An obnoxious shriek interrupted the momentary silence and Camille turned to glare at the bird clinging to his cage door. At a glance, Leo looked more amused than was properly acceptable. Camille stifled the stab of envy. He looked perfect. Even his jeans looked as though they had been pressed just that morning, and the silver earring matched the expensive watch and subtle belt buckle like a set.

"So how is the legendary Simon?" Leo's voice was a smudge short of condescending so Camille ignored the comment. Bad enough he should look so much better than she, worse that he should rub in what he considered her most recent mania.

Leo approached the cage with natural grace and bent close. Simon immediately stopped fidgeting and pinned Leo with one pearl gray eye.

"Hey, birdie. Wanna cracker?" Leo's tone was grating to Camille's aching head, but she held her tongue and watched the exchange. Simon climbed with a nimble beak over foot method to the top of his huge cage until he was almost eye level with Leo. He continued his stare through the maneuver, and his short light gray feathers on his neck stood out like a collar on an Elizabethan ladies dress.

"I think he likes me," Leo said, his face perilously close to the bars.

"He'll nip your nose if he can," Camille warned. "He's puffed up to make him look bigger; he's threatening you."

Leo pulled back slightly. "Bite me, will you?"

"He doesn't know you," Camille said, rummaging through the cabinets for a treat. "Give him the cracker but watch his beak."

Leo looked a little wary, but held the snack for the bird, edging between the side spaced bars. Simon snatched it and began his decent, letting out a clear coo as a thank you.

"See, he's not so bad." Camille put the two mugs on the table and sat down gingerly to avoid jolting her tender head.

Simon continued to his water bowl and dipped the cracker in before holding it in his scaly claw and nibbling around the edges like a dainty lady at tea.

"You have a pet that bites. I'm not so sure of your good

The Parrot Told Me

judgment," Leo said frowning.

"He only bites out of necessity," Camille said grinning. "Or if you irritate him."

"Okay, and how do you make him talk?"

Camille glanced at the bird and lowered her voice. "You want to hear it?"

"Well, yeah," Leo said, his voice lowered and his face comical in its earnestness.

"Come on." Camille ducked out of the kitchen, coffee in hand, and went into the dimmed living room. The late morning light was slanting in through the blinds, sending stripes of color through the gloom. Magazines were tossed about on the couch and the day's paper still tightly rolled lay on the antique trunk in front of the sagging sofa. Camille was mildly embarrassed by the two wine bottles and empty glass that remained on the floor next to her favorite chair, but Leo prudently refrained from comment.

Camille slid behind her desk and pulled out the drawer to rummage through files. In the one labeled "pets", she paged through the vet bills and sundry pamphlets. Her last recorded dictation of the bird's conversation was stapled in a neat sheaf with the pages numbered.

Leo looked impressed when she handed him the papers.

"I wrote word for word what I heard the second time around. He even added a little more to the dialogue that time. I want to make sure and record it as soon as I get a good machine."

"And you said there was music?"

"Yes, the same each time. I think that's the trigger; it sets him off and makes him remember."

"Was Monica a big music fan?"

"Don't know," Camille said, turning to the stereo. "She may have just used this for some sort of mood music. But whatever it was, Simon certainly remembers it."

Leo dropped to the couch and began skimming through the pages, his eyes dark with concentration.

A hollow metal pinging announced Simon's shuffles in the cage and he let out a long wolf whistle.

"Hello," Simon called in his odd birdy voice.

"Hey, Simon," Camille returned, still flipping through the CD titles.

"Happy bird day to you," he chanted, the tune vaguely reminiscent of the Happy Birthday song.

"Pretty Bird, Simon," Camille said absently.

"Are you my Baby bird?" Simon replied, his voice pitched an octave higher.

"That's Monica," Camille said softly, turning to Leo. He had paused in his reading and was facing the kitchen as well. "He talks in a high voice for about half of the time, saying things that I'm sure she said to him."

Leo looked curious. "So he knows the difference in who speaks to him?"

"Sure," Camille responded as Simon continued crooning to himself. "He imitates her voice and mine as well. They sound very different, even though they're both higher pitched. It's her accent that gives her away the most, although the tone of her voice was a different tone, deep really for a woman, and slightly rough."

Leo looked thoughtfully back to the page before him. "So how many other voices does he use?"

"I don't know, really. Everyone once in a while, a new one will crop up that I haven't heard before. But he has about three or four that I hear most. Monica's, mine, and a few men's, one with a really strong accent like Monica's. Most of the phrases are pretty canned; the things that people usually say to the birds. But every so often I'll hear a new greeting or something, and in those voices, it's a little creepy."

"So when he said this," Leo said, holding up the papers, "It was in Monica's voice with her accent?"

"Yeah, mostly, except for the man's voice."

Almost on key, Simon's voice interrupted with a low growl. "Polly want a cracker?"

"Is that it? The man?"

Camille looked up from the CDs and frowned. "I'm not sure, but similar. It's definitely not the guy with the accent."

"Hey, baby. Wanna dance?" Monica's sultry tone was painfully distinct, alive.

"What the..?" Leo looked shocked, unduly so, and Camille studied him for a moment. "Oh man, that's creepy."

61

The Parrot Told Me

"For a man who just 'checked her out', you certainly seem surprised to hear her voice." Leo was looking away and Camille dropped the CD on the trunk. "Hey, is there something you didn't tell me?" She meant it as a joke, but the look on his face wasn't the least bit funny.

"Camille, I…"

"Oh, Leo, you've got to be kidding!"

"No, wait! It wasn't what you think. I had met her before, but it was months ago. She looked different; she was different."

"And what? You got involved and decided not to tell me?"

"No! Not involved so shut up a minute."

Camille fumed as she dropped to the couch, instantly regretting the sudden movement as her headache flared to life. Leo sank down next to her and tugged her socked feet into his lap.

"It wasn't what you think, so stop giving me that look. I met Monica about six months ago at a bar downtown." He paused to pick up his mug and take a sip. "I was dancing, so was she, and we kind of hooked up."

Camille tried to school her features into some semblance of understanding, while her teeth clenched. "Hooked up? That's nice!"

"Hold up," he said quickly. "We danced. We talked. Maybe a little more in a dark corner, but it never left the dance floor. It ended there."

"And you never mentioned it. Why?"

"Look at you! You're just waiting to lunge. When I realized who it was that died, I didn't think it was a good time to speak up. Hell, I didn't even know she was your neighbor until I caught sight of her in the hallway just a few weeks before she died. At that time, avoiding her was my main goal. And then she was gone, and it seemed pretty useless to mention it."

"What about when I told you about my suspicions about Monica's death? About Simon?"

"I didn't want to get into it." He sighed and ran his fingers though his stiff locks. "You were upset. You still are. It just never seemed to fit in the conversation."

Camille huffed and leaned back against the couch, angry but not so much that she could doubt him.

"Fine, fine. So you still think I'm over reacting."

62

"I don't know, Camille. Really, I just haven't decided either way."

They sat in silence, uncomfortable but still together, their friendship a bobbing yo-yo of emotions.

"So you want to hear Simon?"

~*~

The dialogue was perfect, starting precisely at the onset of the music, halting in the flurry of squawks and flapping wings. Leo looked vaguely sick. The bird's rendition was strange enough for Camille, who was accustomed to Simon's split personality sound, but for Leo, it was like a voice from the grave.

"So what do you think now?"

Leo had been silent for a long time, his hand supporting his chin while he gazed into the liquid gold of the wine at the bottom of the bottle.

"Weird," he said, without raising his eyes.

"But do you think it could be?" She left off the rest, not daring to say it aloud.

"Camille, I don't know. I honestly don't know what that was about. But maybe you were right. Maybe we need to find out." He looked at her sternly. "I'm not saying that any of this is for sure, so don't jump to any conclusions yet. I'm just saying that it might be something, and you should watch what you say and do." He frowned at her expression. "I mean it Camille. This isn't a time to be doing anything hasty or stupid."

Camille nodded silently as Simon crooned in the other room.

Chapter 7

Leo's concerned skepticism may have put a mild damper on Camille's determination, but even he could not deny the obvious. The bird had heard a strange dialogue, and the conversation had definitely been between Monica and a man. There was no denying the voices.

Camille's goal now was to figure out who the man had been. The possibilities were endless. Monica had been an attractive, well spoken, and outgoing young woman who apparently, according to rumor, had few qualms regarding who she bedded. The conversation could have involved any number of suspects, very possibly Max, the neighbor upstairs, or at a long-shot, Leo himself.

Camille was tempted to dismiss both men. The conversation, as told by the bird, appeared to be familiar and intimate, not a one night stand kind of dialogue. That relieved Leo of guilt, but Camille's reasons for dismissing Max were less logical. It just didn't feel right. There was something about him that made Camille think that he didn't have it in him to be a murderer. She just hoped her judgment wasn't clouded by any first impression emotions.

With her usual hard headed determination, Camille decided to continue her own private investigation. Her next step was to go to a place where people were likely to have known Monica best, her office.

Nelson and Tower was housed in the heart of downtown Lexington, just a few blocks from the Civic Center and all the festivities of the city. Renovated older buildings rose shoulder to shoulder like tin soldiers, their proud faces hiding the new and updated interiors.

Monica's office was on the second floor with an iffy view of the shaded street below. Camille was greeted by a receptionist who stood guard before a line of regimented cubicles. Faced with the frowning greeting, Camille was tempted to give it up and say she was in the wrong suite. Instead, she forced a smile and strolled up to the woman's desk.

"May I help you?" The stern woman glanced over half glasses

and looked anything but helpful.

"I heard you had a job opening."

The woman's eyebrows rose and her thin lips tightened, squeezing into a pale line of displeasure.

"I don't believe we're hiring."

"I was sure that I saw it in the paper," Camille lied hurriedly.

The woman stayed at her desk, her eyes narrowed. "I think not."

"You can check with someone," Camille said, showing her teeth in a stiff smile.

"I will."

To Camille's relief, the woman disappeared into the deeper recesses of the office, leaving Camille alone. Eager for the opportunity to see some of the other employees, Camille started to slide past the reception desk toward the cubicles. The sound of voices caused her to stop and turn guiltily as the door opened from the hallway. She felt the odd tingle of shock at the sight of the two men and gathered her composure with difficulty as they turned their attention in her direction.

One of them was the man from the portrait. There was no mistaking the silver-polished hair, the burnished profile, or the proud shoulders. Camille would have bet money that beneath that exquisitely cut suit coat and starched shirt, there was a tattoo of a cat.

"Mr. Tower," the receptionist cooed, her voice sliding an octave higher than Camille thought was biologically possible. She took a cautious step back and stood stiffly.

Mr. Tower turned from his companion; a short, squat man built like a mini refrigerator, and fastened his eyes on the shrill woman.

"This woman says she heard we were hiring. I haven't found anything..." the receptionist's voice drifted to silence when the man's blue gaze slid to Camille where she stood frozen by the desk.

"Hiring?" He glanced toward his companion who raised bushy eyebrows and gave a faint shake of dissent. "No, I don't think we're looking right now."

Camille squirmed beneath the pointed gaze and looked back toward the receptionist to avoid facing Tower. "Then I apologize. I must have gotten my addresses mixed up." She felt her face heat at the lie and longed to leave.

"I believe I told you," The receptionist snapped, but was cut off

The Parrot Told Me

by Tower himself.

"If you wish to leave your resume at the desk, we'll keep it for our personnel files in case something opens up." Tower's expression was one of bland indifference and Camille wondered if she had been a man, or better yet, a more seductive woman, if his attitude would be different.

Then again, if the man had been involved with Monica, than he had to have had a fair interest in younger women.

"Thank you," Camille said quickly, giving them both a vague smile. "I'll bring it around soon." When she moved toward the door, Tower and his companion moved aside, highly polished shoes scraping against tasteful tiled floors.

Tower's hand was at the door before Camille could reach it, so she stood back as he swung the door wide. In passing, she noted two things. Mr. Tower smelled very strongly of a very familiar cologne mixed with a subtle smoky scent, and Mr. Tower wore a wide gold wedding band on his left hand.

~*~

Camille wasn't sure why she was surprised that Monica's painted lover had also been her boss. Naive as she was, she knew affairs happened every day. The Catholic in her frowned, but the realist reminded her that there were reasons behind every action.

If Monica had been alive and well, Camille probably would have settled for a raised eyebrow, but death had changed things.

Camille paused, books in hand, to pass a polite smile. Of all the days for Leo to be off, he had to choose this one. Camille was brimming with nerves and anxious to recount her experience at Monica's office. She busied herself with coordinating the work schedule for their few employees and then sat down at the computer to check out the books. It had taken some time, but the place was finally making some money. Camille sighed in relief. It might not be enough for a trip to Hawaii, but it was enough to ease some of Camille's financial worries. Sales were almost booming. At least in comparison to the last two weeks. The author signing the day before had had a lot to do with it, Camille was sure. Although Sue Ellen Manelle wasn't a big name yet, Camille could feel the potential for fame in the air. And she loved casting her support for a local girl, especially one with an obvious talent. They had sold over 40 copies of the debut novel in the last 2 days, and people who came to buy one book often bought more.

Camille didn't feel right, despite the business success. She was in the strangest mood and couldn't force herself to sit down or be still. She didn't know if it was Monica, or her brush with Monica's slight scandal that had caused Camille's spine to prickle.

She closed down the computer and peeked out the office door. Candice was ringing up a couple of teenagers buying glossy magazines, but no one else appeared to be waiting for her. The transaction complete, Candice gave the girls her best motherly smile and adjusted her bifocals with quick efficient movements.

Candice was an ideal employee. Chatty without being intrusive, old enough to mother two teenagers, but fortunate to have some really good kids. Camille hadn't had the slightest problem with Candice and should have felt comfortable watching her handle the next inquiring customer. But she felt that there was something odd about the way the man was standing back, his head angled away from the desk. He was listening in. Camille slowly slipped out of her office and closed the door, her hands feeling slick and cold. What to do? There was no reason to call the police; the man had done nothing outwardly wrong.

Camille ducked back in the office and emerged with her cell phone in her hand. Standing back, she dialed 911 and headed up to the desk and register, her fingers hovering above the "send" button.

The customer at the desk left, leaving Candice facing the stranger as he still stood back, head cocked, an odd smile on his lips.

"Can I help you?"

Camille reached the desk as the man stepped up, his eyes finally focused forward. With a jerky movement, he pulled a note from his pocket and dropped it on the counter. The smiled remained as he turned slowly, his eyes meeting Camille's. He licked his lips in an odd serpentine manner and raised one pale hand. The gesture was like a gun shooting, one finger pointing toward Camille's chest. With a sharp jerk, he pulled the hand back as though jolted from a shot, and dropped his arm.

In silence, he left.

"What was that?" Candice's voice sounded abnormally loud in

The Parrot Told Me

the quiet of the empty store.

"I," Camille swallowed with difficulty. "I don't know. I don't know him, do you?" Camille was moving quickly to the door, pressing her face to the glass to see if she could see his retreating back. But he was gone. She locked the deadlock and hurried back to where Candice was opening the note that he had dropped on the counter.

"Don't!" Camille shouted.

Candice's fingers jerked away, letting the open note flutter to the floor. "What?" Her face looked pale, almost angry.

"Sorry, sorry," Camille said earnestly. "I didn't mean to scare you any more than you are. I just didn't know what that was, or what might be in there. That guy was just too creepy."

"Its fine," Candice returned, although her expression said otherwise.

Camille leaned over and picked up the note, not knowing what she expected, but realizing that it was something that frightened her in a way that few things ever had. She picked up the paper between two fingers and put it on the counter again. With a trembling hand, she unfolded it the rest of the way, spreading it out as best she could without touching anything but the corners.

"Leave it alone," Candice read, leaning over Camille's shoulder. "What the heck does that mean?"

"I don't know," Camille murmured. "I really don't."

Candice looked more closely at Camille. "Are you feeling alright?"

Camille pressed her fingers against her temples, feeling a familiar headache coming on. She breathed in slowly, focusing on the smooth gold of the wooden floor instead of the stark white of the paper before her.

"I'm fine," she said at last, looking into Candice's concerned eyes. "But listen, it's almost four and we're due to close at five. Let's just close up shop now and call it a day. I don't feel comfortable staying open with the strange man out there so close."

"Are you sure? He's surely gone by now, and the note really didn't say anything that threatening."

"Yes, I'm sure. Until I figure out what the note means, I want to be a little more cautious, especially with Leo gone."

"Well, if you're sure, I'll help you close," Candice responded, her soothing voice making Camille smile gratefully.

"I'm positive, and thank you so much for being such a great help."

~*~

Once home, Camille nervously checked her locks for a second time before kicking off her shoes and switching on the TV. The flash and the noise barely held her attention, so she went to her bookshelf and grabbed a paperback she had been meaning to get to for a week. With a frown she rubbed her fingers over the shiny cover. Her fingerprints left soft smudges and she found herself distracted by the pattern. What kind of fingerprints would they have found in Monica's apartment if they hadn't dismissed it as accident?

"Are you my baby bird?" Simon demanded from the kitchen.

"Hi, Simon," Camille returned, dropping the book on the couch. "You want a cracker?" She wondered into the kitchen and pulled out the large plastic box stowed beneath the side board. She lifted it onto the table and pulled off the lid. Inside was a variety of bird food, from pellets to seeds, dried fruits, nuts, and other goodies. A jumble of bird toys lay to the side, tucked beneath the bag of items she had taken from Monica's apartment. She hadn't even opened the bag since she had brought it home. So much for the insistence that the bird needed the things. She had made a liar out of herself.

With a grimace she pulled out the bag and dumped the contents on her wooden table, a half dozen plastic cubes scattering across the polished surface. There was a set of wooden sticks that resembled nothing so much as colored tongue depressors, several small cups in primary colors, some long sticks that looked like chopsticks, and a variety of perches with toys strung together on leather laces and wooden beads.

Camille stood and swung open the big cage door while Simon eyed her suspiciously. He was used to her presenting treats to entice him out. He crept down to the doorway and studied her before climbing beak over foot to the top of the cage.

Camille grabbed up an almond and presented it to him, shell and

The Parrot Told Me

all. He took it gingerly in his beak and worked on breaking it open. While he wrestled with his treat, she separated out the items on the table and studied them curiously. She was used to some of the small toys that she gave Casey, her smaller bird. The cockatiel wasn't really that interested in toys, but would chew on some of them occasionally. These were much larger, heavier and chunkier. She fingered the set of sticks, then slowly separated the items into little piles.

Simon, abandoning the half eaten nut, skittered over to where she was sorting the toys and halted, watching her with keen interest.

"Now what were you doing here?" she asked idly. She pushed at one of the wooden cubes. "Do you carry these around or just chew on them?"

Simon stepped closer and nudged one of the blocks with his beak.

"Pretty blue," she said fingering a few of the other blocks. "I think I like the yellow one." She glanced at the bird, who had moved on to the orange block. "No, I like the yellow one," she said, grinning as the bird skittered closer. He gave her one keen look and ducked to pick up the yellow cube.

"Yep, that's the one," she said smiling, and watched as he carried it close to her. With a speculative look, she put out her hand, palm up. "Can you give it to me?"

"Yellow," he replied, and dropped the block in her hand.

"Good Grief," she exclaimed, taking the block. "Do you really know these?" More deliberately, she spread out the blocks. "Get the blue one, Simon."

Immediately, as though playing a much loved game, Simon picked up the blue block and carried it to her, waiting patiently until she put out her hand to take it from him.

They tried over and over with Simon choosing the correct colored block almost every time. After a few minutes, Camille noticed that Simon was looking distractedly at the counter and followed his gaze.

"Nuts!" she said, grinning. "You want an almond?"

The bird waited patiently until she picked up the bag, and Simon took the offered nut carefully. After he had shredded the shell and devoured the nut, he crept up to her and hooted fondly.

"Good bird," she said gently, and when she raised her hand, he ducked his head so she could stroke the feathers there and on his neck.

"Are you my baby bird?" he asked in a gentle voice, causing Camille to smile again.

"Getting tired, are you?" she asked. She put out her hand and gave him the command to step up, pleased when he immediately responded. "Good boy," she praised, and put her hand with the bird clinging to her fingers in his massive cage. Obediently, the bird stepped onto his perch and turned around to look at her. After giving him one more nut, she closed the cage door and scooped up the toys. His talents were surprising and intriguing. Apparently Monica had spent a great deal of time with the bird in order to train him so well. She had only heard of birds that had learned how to identify objects or colors, and she certainly had never seen one. It was no surprise that the bird would take the loss of his owner so hard, down to memorizing her last words. With a speculative glance at her feathered roommate, she opened her laptop computer and pulled up a search engine.

"Bird training," she said aloud, and started a search.

The Parrot Told Me

Chapter 8

"Hey, anybody home?"

Camille ducked her head out of the kitchen and waved to Leo. She had the heavy metal bottom pulled out of the bird's cage and was scrubbing energetically.

"Ugh. I knew there was a reason I didn't have any pets," Leo's face was creased with disgust.

"You just can't abide any mess, animal or human," Camille responded, rinsing the tray with clear water.

"Could be right," Leo agreed, and plucked an apple from the bowl on the table. He ate, leaning against the counter, watching Camille as she finished the chore.

Simon watched her as well, plastered to the ceiling of the cage, a suspicious eye following every move of Camille's hand. She had found that he was particularly protective of the territory, and she moved with caution. He hadn't bit at her yet, but had fluffed up his feathers and made some fairly threatening postures.

"He looks at a real sweetheart right now," Leo commented, gesturing with his apple to the stressed bird.

"He just doesn't like me messing with his cage. He's really great when he's out." She closed the cage door and stepped back, pleased when Simon climbed back to his perch and hooted gently. "It was amazing. You should have seen the things that he could do. And when I looked it up on the computer, I found whole groups who concentrate on training birds, some for entertainment, some for safety, and some for science."

"And you said he knows shapes and colors?"

"And more," Camille enthused. "He knows different foods, objects. I had him out yesterday to practice and the darn thing followed me to the bathroom and said 'tub, tub'. I think Monica must have bathed him in there at some point. He puffed up and stretched out like he thought he was going into a rain shower."

72

"So you've figured out that the bird is smart and knows a lot about your apartment."

"Well, since Monica's apartment is the same lay out as mine, it could be that he just recalls the floor plan. Or he might have heard the water running and just followed the noise."

"Does this back up your theory that the bird was quoting a real event?" Leo asked, one eyebrow raised as he tossed the apple core into the trash.

"Knowing that he was very intelligent and highly trained does make me think that it's more likely that what he says is real. He was really bonded with Monica. It just seems more likely that he would recall what she said."

Leo nodded and bent down to look eye to eye with the bird. Simon came slowly to the side of the cage, pinning Leo with one gray eye, his pupil expanding and contracting. His feathers fluffed and he produced a loud clicking noise.

"Good birdie?" Leo said, his voice a little less certain.

"Not just now," Camille said, amused at the interaction.

Leo jumped visibly when a loud knock sounded at the door. "Son of a –," Leo muttered, and backed away from the cage, one hand over his heart. "Were you expecting anyone?"

"No," Camille replied slowly, moving into the living room and approaching the door. She paused and tiptoed to look through the peep hole. "It's Max," she said, turning back to Leo as he leaned on the doorframe between the kitchen and the living room.

A second sharp knock had her flipping the deadbolt and pulling open the door.

"Hey," Max said, his voice pitched low. "I just got a note from the landlady saying that she wanted Monica's key back. I had a feeling that you might want to take a second look around before she has the place cleaned out." He dug into a jean pocket and pulled out the key sans the fuzzy dice. "I thought I'd..." His voice died when he spotted Leo standing in the doorway of the kitchen.

"Come in," Camille commanded, and stepped back.

Max looked uncomfortable, but stepped inside obediently. Camille quickly shut the door after him and locked the door again.

"I thought your best advice was for me to drop this thing,"

The Parrot Told Me

Camille said sounding faintly bitter, facing Max.

"Have you? Dropped it, I mean?" Max gave her a half smile that softened his features into something much more approachable. "I figured that you weren't likely to leave it alone, so I decided that I'd give you one more chance. Just in case you were right."

"I am right, and I feel more and more certain." Camille crossed her arms over her college tee shirt and wished she had done something with her hair. Being well groomed would have at least made her look more credible. Instead, she looked like an out of work college student.

"Yeah, well, maybe now you can prove it." Max had the key in his hand, but didn't offer it to her. His eyes went back to Leo and stayed there.

"Oh, sorry." Camille turned and gestured to Leo. "Max, this is my friend and business partner, Leo. Leo, my doubtful neighbor, Max."

Leo nodded. They both appeared to be sizing each other up, and Camille felt tension build. What was it with men?

The tension was abruptly broken when Simon crooned in his best Monica voice, "Hey, big boy, come on in."

Max visibly cringed, and Leo looked equally as uneasy.

"Damn, that is creepy. Don't know if I'll ever get used to that." Max looked at Camille.

Camille agreed on principle, but had gotten used to the voice, and she cast him a wry smile.

"Yeah, and just how well did you know Monica?" Leo's voice was challenging, and Camille slipped between the two men.

"We were neighbors. Nothing more. But I heard her voice a lot. The walls here aren't great for keeping the sound down, and Monica had visitors at all hours. I work at night, so I tend to hear what goes on during the day."

"I know it's true about the walls," Camille agreed. "I hear my neighbors moving around, even when I know they are trying to be quiet. Did you ever hear who Monica was talking to?"

Max looked uncomfortable and shifted his weight from one booted foot to the other. "It's not my place to repeat what I heard over there. Not good to speak ill of the dead and all of that. I just know that Monica had her fair share of male attention."

Camille nodded, suddenly impatient. "We know that Monica had lots of boyfriends. That is a given. I just wonder if there was anyone who might have been angry or jealous enough to want to kill her."

Neither man had an answer for that one. Camille turned back into the kitchen and they followed at a distance. With a frown, Camille looked back at Simon hovering in the corner of the cage. She found one of his favorite blocks of wood and slipped it inside the cage. While he was chewing on it tentatively, Camille finished cleaning the cage and closed the door securely. With the extra people in the room, Simon had decided he didn't really want to speak any longer, but couldn't resist throwing out a few hopeful whistles when Camille got out his pellet bag.

"Let me feed Simon and then we'll go on up. Are we sure that Mrs. Patterson isn't home?"

Max nodded and stood back while Camille poured the bird pellets into Simon's shiny metal dish. "I saw her leave a few minutes ago. That's why I decided to come down here. I know she would be royally pissed if she knew we were going in there. She doesn't like anyone to mess around with the apartments, and said that if Monica's family doesn't come and get her stuff by the end of the month, she's going to get rid of it herself."

"Can she do that?" Camille asked, appalled.

"If the rent is due, and Monica didn't pay up for next month, I guess she can. If no one is there to complain, it's really her building to do with as she pleases."

Camille put away the bird pellets and ushered the men into the living room again. "Just let me grab my shoes and we'll go," she said, and headed toward the bedroom.

The men were silent as she slipped on her sandals and hurried back out to the living room. She closed the door behind them and locked it, even though they were only going to be gone for a few minutes. She no longer felt safe in her own building, and she found that she was saddened by the fact. She had always liked the apartment building, even with all of its quirks. She could just hope that they would get something solved soon so that she could go back to feeling safe again.

Upstairs, she almost laughed at the picture they must have made. She led with Max close behind and Leo walking at a distance, trying, it seemed, to look like he wasn't part of the group. Camille noticed that going down the hall; he walked with a lighter tread and wondered if he

The Parrot Told Me

were worried about running into Chloe again.

At Monica's floor, Camille stepped back and let Max use the key to open the lock. The apartment was just as she had seen it before, except now the dead flowers had been removed and the room smelled much better for it. She also noticed that the painting in the front room was uncovered, and went by herself down the hall to see if the other one was uncovered as well. The portrait stood as it had earlier, still covered by the tarp. Camille walked over and uncovered it herself, pausing a moment to admire the fine workmanship. With her second viewing, she was even surer that she had met the subject of the portrait. Monica had captured, not just the physical likeness of the man, but something of the way he held himself, the confident air, and the subtlety of posture. He was a man secure in his own skin, and he radiated this through the brushstrokes of the painting.

Had Monica loved him? For a moment, Camille was overcome with a sense of sadness. It seemed impossible that someone would render a subject in such emotional detail and not harbor some feelings for them. And if she had loved him, would she have demanded more? She had the reputation for being a woman not satisfied with just one relationship, but if she had truly fallen in love with someone, might she have decided to change her ways?

But Mr. Tower was married. Although the portrait definitely didn't show it, Camille had seen his heavy gold band, and knew that at least for now, he was married and openly showing it. If Monica had threatened that relationship, or even given the hint of telling his wife, would he have found it necessary to shut her up in some way?

Camille was unaware of anyone coming up behind her until she felt the pressure of a hand on her shoulder. Expecting Leo, she was surprised to see Max standing there.

"Sorry, you seemed too lost in thought. I called your name twice, and you didn't seem to hear me."

She nodded, but admitted that she was feeling a little disassociated, as through her thoughts had taken on more reality than her surroundings. "I was thinking," she said vaguely.

"About him?" Max asked, nodding his head toward the painting.

"Maybe," Camille replied, and followed his gaze to the portrait. "Do you know who it is?"

76

Rachael Rawlings

"One of her guys, I guess," he said, his voice casual and unconcerned. "He doesn't look familiar, but that doesn't surprise me. I didn't meet any of them, and often times Monica had visitors while I was at work. I would see them leaving in the morning when I was coming in." He looked toward the portrait, and then back at Camille. "You recognize him, don't you?"

Camille nodded, unable to keep the truth from her expression. "He was her employer," she said softly.

Leo came up behind her and stopped abruptly. "Hey, you should see the painting in the front room. It's amazing. She was really good."

Camille turned to face him, grateful to be distracted from the portrait. "She had tons of other pieces in here too. She had plenty to be in a show, and most of her work is really impressive." She felt a wave of pity come over her, and she sighed. "It's such a sad thing. She could have really been successful."

"She was on her way," Max said offhandedly, looking through one of the many stacks of canvases. He glanced up to see Leo and Camille looking at him expectantly. "She had finally gotten a big show. She was supposed to be traveling to Chicago this spring. One of her smaller studio shows had gotten some big reviews, and a friend of a friend had hooked her up with someone who was pulling some strings. She was really excited about it." His face reflected a remembered sadness, as though he were recalling her death all over again. "Wonder what they will do about the show now?"

Camille looked at the paintings, so alive even in the half light. "Maybe they will host the show posthumously. Mara might know, although I'm not eager to talk with her again."

"You?" Max's face was incredulous. "She didn't just rake you over the coals!"

Leo looked from one to the other and smiled wryly. "Maybe I need to meet this lady."

Camille ignored him and walked out of the guest-room. The hallway smelled faintly musty, the air not moving. She entered the master bedroom and stood for a moment in the doorway. Something was different in here. She knew someone had been in the apartment since her last visit. Someone had taken out the rotting flowers, and probably checked to make sure everything was working properly in the kitchen.

77

The Parrot Told Me

Mrs. Patterson? She seemed to be the most likely candidate. She had to have been in from time to time anyway, getting the bird out, for one. Had anyone else been in?

"Hey, we probably need to hurry this up a little," Max said from behind her, his steps loud in the carpeted hallway.

"When was the last time you were in here?" Camille asked, turning toward him.

"Not for a few weeks, just after Monica died. I came in to check over the place after the police had gone. I don't really like being in here much. I guess I've avoided thinking about it too much. Why?"

"Some things have been moved," Camille replied, gesturing to the bedroom. "I know the bed covers have been shifted around, and I know some of those clothes weren't on the floor when I came in earlier."

"Probably Mrs. Patterson or someone looking at cleaning the place out," Max responded, but he didn't look happy. "I really can't wait until this is all shipped out. It looks like Monica was just here yesterday."

Camille had to agree, but she still had the odd feeling of wrongness. Something was out of place, and she couldn't exactly put her finger on it. She went around Max and into the doorway of the bathroom. It too had been disturbed. The curtain around the tub had been pulled back, and the towels that had so neatly been folded in the cabinet were piled in stacks on the tiled floor. The candles had been moved from their perch on the window sill, and were thrown in the sink. Obviously whoever had been in here had little regard for Monica's things.

Max had come up behind Camille and was looking over her shoulder. After a moment, she heard the soft step of Leo as he came in after them. When he ducked into the bathroom as well, he looked at Camille curiously.

"So, what's up? What are you thinking?"

Camille faced the two men, her back to the room and its obvious disorder. "I think someone has been in there looking for something. The bedroom was disturbed, and this bathroom has definitely had someone searching through it. When I was here earlier, there was nothing out of place. And I guess whoever did this just assumed that no one else could be in here to see what they had left behind. I guess they just thought that someone would be in to pack up Monica's things and wouldn't notice if her belongings had been gone through."

Leo walked into the bathroom and gingerly stepped over the pile of towels. His eyes were sharp and focused as he looked over the room. "What's different?"

Camille briefly described the changes that she had seen in the bathroom as well as the bedroom. As she looked around, she noticed a few other minor discrepancies, and shook her head sadly. It seemed that Monica would not get any respect in death either. After a few minutes, the little group returned to the front room and Camille went into the kitchen. The disorder was less here, except for the desk, which was piled with papers and debris. It looked as if someone had cleaned out the cabinets above and below and stacked the contents in an untidy heap. The phone list was still where Camille had seen it earlier, but this time she was looking more carefully at the business cards pinned to the cork around it.

One definitely stood out. A red circle had been drawn around the first name on a card labeled Nictor Studio. Camille took a moment to read the card aloud.

"That's the place she was going to have her show," Max added, and came to stand beside Camille. Up close, he seemed bigger and more imposing. She backed away from the board, feeling the thrill of nerves tracing up her spine. She was really getting spooked. The heavy air, the slight scent of a female's perfume, and the sight of all Monica's abandoned belongings were getting to her.

"I think I've seen enough," she said grimly. "I don't see anything to help Monica here." Someone had been there. Someone had cared enough to go through Monica's things and look for some type of evidence. If Max had thought bringing her here and letting her look through the apartment again was going to change her mind, he was really wrong on that account.

~*~

Max left them after locking up, stating that he was going to drop the key off for Mrs. Patterson before he did anything else. He was working later, and Camille could see that he was getting the rather abstracted air of someone with a lot on his mind. They told him goodbye, and Leo and Camille headed out the door. They weren't working. The

The Parrot Told Me

shop would have to do with a skeleton crew for one day, and Camille knew that she could do with the rest. But they both had difficulty staying away. With a silent agreement, they rode by the bookstore and stopped inside just to check. The young college girl covering the store was at the cash register, immersed in a mystery book that sat open next to her. The young guy that they had hired to do some of the shelving and heavy lifting was in the back with some of the new stock. The bookstore looked open and welcoming, the smell of freshly made coffee rising above the scent of ink and fresh paper.

"Things going okay?" Camille asked her employee. The girl nodded her ascent, and went back to reading her book. She was cheap because she did little but the minimum, but she was a friend of the family, and dependable to open the store, keep the coffee on, and make sales.

After seeing that the store was running at its usual pace, Leo drove Camille to his tidy apartment where they settled on his couch. They had some work discussion to complete, a regular meeting that they had once a week to discuss how the sales were and if the finances were going as planned. Camille could tell that Leo was eager to drop the shop talk.

"You remember that number from the studio?" he asked. When Camille nodded, he handed her his cell phone and she obediently dialed in the digits. She handed the phone back to him so that he could have his conversation. She wasn't sure what the purpose of the call was, but sat next to him to overhear the conversation.

After a quick ten minutes, Leo hung up, with apparent satisfaction on his face.

"They were hosting the show. It's been cancelled, and they haven't even spoken to anyone about a reschedule date. They were very sorry about what they heard happened to Monica. They had only met her once." Leo paused and took a breath. "But it was going to be a big deal for her career. If this show had been successful, it's pretty likely that she would have had a follow up with their sister studio in New York. From there, the sky would have been the limit."

"And you think her success could have been a motive?"

"I don't know about that exactly, but it does smell of money, possible professional jealously, or even jealously of a lover who is being dumped. Could be a lot of things."

Camille nodded and put her feet up on his coffee table, a slick glass number that would show prints. She grinned at him and smoothed the hair back from her forehead. "So what did you think of neighbor Max?" she asked playfully.

Chapter 9

Mondays had a way of pulling all the weight of the following week, and strapping it to your feet like manacles. Camille felt like she had been at work for hours, when she knew that only an hour had passed. The store was nearly empty. The sole visitor was an elderly lady who had chosen a mystery from the shelves, poured herself a cup of coffee, and sunk into one of the armchairs. Camille had seen her before and knew her type. She would choose a book, read the first few chapters, and if she liked it, she might buy it. On the other hand, if she wasn't happy about the way the plot was going, or the writer's personal style, she would leave the book on a nearby table to be shelved. Either way, she got a free cup of coffee and a few hours of quiet reading in, at least once a week.

Camille would have preferred to be alone. She had a mild headache, and the wind had kicked up, threatening rain. She had her own cup of coffee in front of her, and was glancing through the newspaper when the door opened and her eyes were automatically drawn up.

Mara. There was no mistaking the sour expression, the confident walk, the sheer presence of the woman. Why she had tracked her down, Camille wasn't sure. At a guess from the expression on Mara's face, Camille could tell this was not going to be a friendly visit. Mara looked furious.

"I told you to leave this alone," Mara hissed as soon as she had reached the polished wood counter. She planted her fists on the wood and leaned in close. "I told you not to get involved. Now I find out that you are breaking into Monica's apartment, and you even came to my work!"

Camille flinched, but stood firm. "I came by your work for just a few minutes, and I didn't mention you or Monica."

"Did you think that they didn't notice anything about your visit? I saw you in there fumbling around. They were trying to figure out who you were."

"But still. That didn't have anything to do with Monica," Camille argued.

"Let me put it this way. Mr. Tower knows where you live. He knows that you are in the same building as Monica. He's asking questions of a lot of people. He's suspicious."

Camille felt herself blanch a little. He had certainly looked like a man that she wouldn't want to tangle with. And if the wedding ring was any indication, he was also someone who had something to hide. Something that would be pretty important to his future happiness. Just Camille's presence could have given him the idea that she was checking up on him, if for nothing but the possibility of an affair.

"Do you figure you're the only one that ever thought of blackmail?"

Mara's voice pulled Camille back from her thoughts. "Blackmail? Are you serious? Do you think I'm going to blackmail Mr. Towers? I don't care who he sleeps with, I just wanted to know what happened to Monica!" Then Mara's words really sank in. "What do you mean the only one? Was Monica trying to blackmail him? Is that what the painting was for?"

Mara signed and backed away slightly, her arms going to her sides. She suddenly looked older, and more sad than angry. "I don't know if Monica ever thought of really blackmailing him. I know that she wanted more than he wanted to give, but I don't think she would do anything so stupid. And I saw the painting, so did you. Does it look like revenge to you?"

"No," Camille agreed slowly, "it looked like she just may have had serious feelings for him. The painting was beautiful."

"Her work was beautiful," Mara said, and turned to look out the plate glass window, her eyes blind to the scene in front of her. "She was so talented, and she was so anxious to throw it all away."

For a moment, Camille was sure that Mara was close to breaking down. Her face had lost that set and angry look, and her shoulders had curved in, vulnerable, like a child. But before she could really give any response, Mara turned back to her, her damp eyes now blazing. "You just leave her alone. She doesn't deserve her reputation to be dragged through the mud for your enjoyment. I'm not warning you again."

The Parrot Told Me

Camille leaned back, away from the woman's hot gaze and labored breath. Mara was frightening when she looked like that. Her cheeks were flushed in an unhealthy way, and her lips clinched as though she were holding something distasteful in her mouth. But she said no more. She turned and marched to the door, yanking it open with too much force, and stepping through without so much as a backward glance.

~*~

When Leo came in an hour later, Camille had gone to the bakery next door and bought the biggest, gooiest doughnut she would find. She had refreshed her coffee and was drowning her sorrows in chocolate and caffeine. Leo looked from her plate to her face and dropped his things on the counter.

"What happened to you?" he asked, sliding onto a stool and fixing her with that obnoxious brother look.

She told him about Mara's visit, and her conclusions. She found herself unconsciously playing with her earrings and forced her hand down.

"I can't imagine how she thought I could blackmail anyone. The painting only proves that Monica knew him, and everyone who worked there knew that."

Leo looked skeptical. "Sure, but you don't paint that picture of your employer unless you're getting some type of fringe benefits." He gathered his jacket back in his arms and shook his head. "That is one woman you are going to have to avoid. She must have really cared for Monica, and she seems willing to back up her words."

Camille agreed, but had no idea how she could convince Mara that she had no desire to hurt Monica's memory in any way. Leo came back from the office with his own coffee and a stack of envelopes. "Back to work," he said, with mock severity. "You need to drop this for a while, Cammy. Get your mind on something else." Camille nodded, but her heart wasn't in it. She was still thinking of secrets, and what secrets Monica might have had that helped her to her grave.

~*~

That evening, she opened Simon's cage and waited for him to climb onto the top of the cage before she offered him a nut. He whistled a thank you, and sat watching her as she fixed her dinner. She had gotten used to his chattering and his noise, and let him out to wander around the top of the cage each evening. She hadn't been brave enough to try to pick him up often, although she had gently stroked his head when he bent it regally to offer a pet. When the pasta was done, she took her plate to the table and made up a smaller plate for the bird, complete with his own pasta, sauce, and bread.

With more confidence than she felt, she approached the cage and held up her hand. "Step up," she said, offering the universal command to step onto someone's hand.

Immediately, Simon obeyed his training and lifted a foot. When she moved her hand closer, he stepped onto the side of her hand and whistled a loud salute.

"Good bird," Camille murmured, and took him over to the table. When she sat down, she put her hand down to the table next to his plate. Simon gingerly stepped onto the smooth surface of the table and sat looking at her closely, his feather's slightly ruffled. She picked up her fork and tried a bite of her meal, exclaiming aloud how good it was to encourage the bird to try his own. He again looked at her and took a hesitant step toward her.

"What do you want, Bird?" she asked, pausing with her fork suspended.

He let out a piercing whistle and tilted his head, looking into her plate as he shuffled closer. She held still, watching his movements with amusement. He was a little scared still, but curious, and she thought maybe he was starting to trust her. She forked another bite of the pasta and ate it slowly, watching him as he watched her. He stopped at the edge of her plate and leaned down, catching a string of spaghetti in his beak. Balancing on one foot, he used the other to manipulate his treat, and soon had red sauce liberally spread on his scaly feet, his beak, and a few droplets on his chest.

"Do you like it?" Camille asked, moving her hands slowly to avoid startling him.

"Good Bird, have a bite Simon," he responded, his voice pitched in Monica's silky smooth tones. Camille stifled a shiver at the familiar voice, but tore off a piece of her bread and presented it.

"Monica sure spoiled you, didn't she?" she asked him as he leaned over and took the bread gingerly from her fingers.

"Oh, you're Monica's sweet baby," he cooed, his head cocked as though hearing a voice from somewhere above.

"Monica's baby," Camille said softly, and gently stroked the creature's head. His feathers ruffled and his eyes narrowed in a contented expression.

"You be a good boy," he said, allowing her to pet him.

Camille hesitated at her mail box and unlocked the door. Her usual collection of junk mail was stacked neatly, slightly rolled to fit into the snug confines of the space. On the top was a magazine, glossy and bright, with a flashy blue and red parrot on the front, hanging from an elaborate rope swing. She shook her head and a small smile touched her lips. This really was the reason she had ended up with Simon. A magazine like this one had drawn Monica's attention and started their first conversation. It was in the heat of the summer, and the door to the front of the building was propped open to allow a breeze from the shaded street out front. While at the mailboxes, Camille had stood beside the reed thin figure of her neighbor and pulled out a bundle of correspondence from her box. Monica's eyes had caught a glimpse of the catalogue featuring bird toys, cages, and other supplies.

"You have a bird?" Monica had asked, interest plain in her eyes.

"Yes, a cockatiel," Camille had responded, surprised at Monica's interest. She had barely spoken more than an offhanded greeting before that day.

"I have an African Grey!" Monica had exclaimed, clearly pleased. It was the most animated that Camille could remember ever seeing Monica.

"Oh," Camille couldn't help but smile. "I thought I had heard a bird in the building, especially last spring when I left the windows open. He talks, doesn't he?"

"That was Simon," Monica had responded, her voice like a doting mother. "He is a smart one. He has a vocabulary that you wouldn't believe, and he's constantly learning more. He's like a little sponge!" Camille had been amused as Monica had then gone on the mention the extreme sensitivity, intelligence, and general brilliance of her pet.

Camille had listened indulgently, startled that Monica was so obviously a "bird" person, when she looked so very, well, different. But it was obvious that Monica had loved the creature, and every time they would meet in the hall, Camille would go out of her way to ask about the bird, and was always treated to several "Simon" stories.

Now Camille tucked the magazine under her arm and turned to go up the stairs. She had reached the first turn in the stairs when she heard the distinct sound of someone opening the front door. She paused to see if it might be Max. Instead, the unmistakable figure of Mr. Tower stepped into the small entryway. Camille, panicked, ducked down the hall, and hurried to her door. With nervous fingers, she thrust the key in the lock and managed to throw open the door just as heavy footfalls sounded at the head of the stairs. She closed the door behind her as quickly and as quietly as she could. In the dim light of her own apartment, she huddled against the door and listened for any more footsteps. It was quiet in the hall. He had gone on up. Did he plan to go to Monica's apartment? Did he have a key? Or was he planning on searching her out, looking for the one who had been checking out Monica's past and her untimely passing?

Camille's stomach was rolling as she stepped back from her door and waited for the knock. She felt incredibly stupid for ever getting involved in anything like this. It was as though she felt that with the death of her sister, she should have a pass on tragedy. That somehow, living through that time in her life, she had earned immunity to any harm that might befall any normal person.

She dumped her purse out on the kitchen counter and pulled out a can of pepper spray she had gotten a year ago from her father, and her cell phone. Who to call? Leo was too far away, as were her parents. The police would arrest her for sheer stupidity if she called and said that it was possible that her neighbor's lover was coming to her apartment to do unspeakable things to her. The phone book lay abandoned on the counter so she scooped it up. It was a local listing so it took only a moment to find Max's number. She didn't hesitate, but dialed, and listened anxiously while the phone rang. He might be working. He could

The Parrot Told Me

be sleeping. He might be…

"Hello?" Max's voice sounded rough with sleep or aggravation, but it was a remarkably sweet sound to Camille.

"He's here," she burst out. "Mr. Tower is here in the building. I don't know if he's going upstairs to Monica's apartment or if he wants to talk to me."

There was a pause as Max apparently gathered his thoughts. "Camille? What the hell are you talking about? And why are you whispering? Are you at home?"

"Yes," she hissed. "I'm at home, and I don't know if Mr. Tower is outside my door. I saw him come in the front. He might be headed your way."

On the other end there was the sound of movement and then the clatter of chains as the lock was disengaged. After what seemed like hours, she heard the door close softly and the lock reset. "He's next door," Max said, sounding more awake. "The door is open just a crack. I can't tell what he's doing, but I think we both know what he might be after."

Camille let out the breath she didn't know she had been holding. Tower's presence in the building suddenly made the whole scare very real. "Okay," she said softly, and slumped down in her chair.

"I hear more noises. I'll call you back in a minute." Max hung up before she could protest, although she wasn't sure what she would have said. She set down her cell phone and left it out on the counter while she hung her purse on the customary hook and tucked the pepper spray into her pocket. She shook off her nerves and got up to make herself some coffee. She needed something to do with her hands before Max called back, and she didn't want to just sit by the phone and wait. As the coffee burped and gurgled its way into the pot, she paced the room, putting out sugar and cream, and laying out a spoon which she paused to polish on the dish towel. She peered into Simon's cage and watched him in silence where he sat huddled in the back, one foot up in the midst of a nap. Hours and days passed in her mind, until she heard the brisk rap of knuckles on her door. She dropped the spoon, her heart thudding up to her throat, and was tempted to just stay in place, pretend she wasn't home. With quiet steps, she approached her own door and tiptoed to look out the peep hole. She half expected to see Mr. Tower standing there, disheveled and angry,

88

maybe holding an ax or other lethal instrument. Instead, Max stood shifting uneasily from foot to foot. She slid open the lock and pulled the door open just a crack, peering out to make sure he was alone.

"It's fine. He just left the building a few minutes ago."

She opened to door wider and let him into the apartment, shutting it after her and engaging the lock quickly. "Where did he go?"

"I don't know where he's headed now, but I know he was moving fast. He had something in a big brown wrapper, and at a guess, I'd say he took his painting. He wasn't there long enough to have gone through too much of the apartment."

Camille wandered into the kitchen, frowning. "If he took the portrait, there is no other good evidence linking him to Monica," she said, thinking aloud.

"You're assuming there was something to link him to. It might have been no more than what it looked like, a quick affair between two consenting, if not honest, adults." Max followed her into the kitchen and sniffed appreciatively. "Have any extra coffee?"

While she poured them a mugful, and they added cream and sugar in companionable silence, Camille thought about the passing day. Monica's belongings would be gone soon, and the only thing to tie her into the past would be Simon. What if the whole thing had been a mistake? What if Monica, while making some bad decisions in her personal life, had suffered from a tragic accident and died? Could Camille's quest for the truth be something that only she could see?

Max sat at the table and Camille sat opposite from him, studying his face. He looked tired. She guessed that he had worked the night shift, and she was seeing the accumulated fatigue from it on his face. His hair was pulled back, but there was a definite shadow marking his jaw. His hair actually looked a little damp, and Camille wondered how much sleep he had gotten. She felt guilty looking at him. He probably had come home, showered, and had barely fallen asleep before she had called and disturbed him. And for what? He had seen Tower leave with a portrait that no man would want just laying around.

"I'm sorry for waking you. I just suddenly had this feeling that he might be coming for me, and I needed to call someone for backup. You were the closest."

Max sighed and took a sip of his coffee. "Thanks, I guess. It's

The Parrot Told Me

okay that you called me. I can always sleep later." He wrapped his big hands around the mug, warming himself. "I don't know what to think about Monica. I know that she sometimes could be a little rash and emotional, but I can't imagine her driving anyone far enough that they would want to kill her. It just doesn't make sense. Even if Tower wanted to shut her up, there seems to be a lot of less violent ways to do it."

"You're right," Camille said, resting her chin in her hand. "Maybe I'm just making too much of this. Monica was young, and it seems so wrong that she is dead. It seems so useless." She stirred her coffee aimlessly, watching the liquid swirl lazily in the cup. "I hate when things don't make sense, and when Simon started saying things, I felt like he was trying to communicate something to me."

"Simon? What do you mean?"

Camille felt her face flush when she realized what she had let slip. She had had no intention of ever letting Max know just how crazy she was to have taken the birds words so seriously. But now the proverbial cat was out of the bag.

"Simon said something that made me think Monica had been fighting with someone." Camille looked at his face expecting disbelief. Instead, he just looked interested.

"Okay, what did he say?"

They both turned to look at Simon, who was awake but silent on his perch. Camille felt of surge of something close to anger at the bird. Even though none of this was his fault, she felt foolish for listening to him. She felt somehow betrayed both by her own beliefs, and by him. "Dumb bird," she muttered, and looked back into her coffee.

"Pasta time?" Simon asked. Then in that warm southern draw, "Monica's sweet baby."

"I don't know. That is awfully convincing. He sounds just like her." Max got up and leaned closer to the cage. "What do you know, Bird?"

But when no food was offered, Simon retreated to the back of his cage and started a soft cooing. He had said what he wanted, and typical of his breed, spoke only when he chose.

Max sat back down in his chair across from Camille and studied the bird for a few minutes. "What exactly did he say?"

"You mean, when he was imitating Monica?"

Max nodded. "It must have been something strange to make you think Monica had been murdered."

She stood and went past him to the small desk. Inside were all of her important papers, stacked haphazardly. She pulled out her notebook and turned it over to show him the pages she had written out. He took it silently and read, his eyes studying the words while his brow lowered in thought.

"I can't imagine what this might mean. I guess until we find out more about what happened to Monica, we won't really know what he was talking about. But you think that this was Monica talking to her killer."

"I think it could be. I think Simon heard something said with such emotion that he remembered it exactly."

Max looked thoughtful. "Monica did say that he had learned curse words after just hearing them one time. She told me that of her friends said something in front of him and he immediately picked it up. I guess she didn't want me to think she was teaching him that kind of thing." He rubbed his hand warily over his face. "She was funny about some things."

"You're tired, and I'm keeping you up," Camille said apologetically.

"I'm fine," he said, but interrupted himself with a yawn. "I am glad you told me about this. It gives me something to think about. Especially on those long shifts."

"You work all night?"

"Yeah, I work out at the airport, the nightshift." He sat up, propping his elbows on the table and scrubbing his face with callused fingers. "This schedule's going to get the best of me eventually. I'm not meant to be a night owl."

"I couldn't stand it," Camille agreed, eyeing him steadily.

"I heard you owned a bookstore," Max said, angling back. "Sounds like a lot of work."

"It was for a while," she agreed. "Leo and I almost drove ourselves in the ground trying to get the place ready. But we've got a great location and facility. It's getting easier."

"By easier, you mean 40 hour weeks."

Camille smiled and brushed her fingers through her hair. "Not quite. That might take retirement."

The Parrot Told Me

Max nodded slowly. "I know what you mean. I keep wanting to fly more, get certified on some bigger crafts, but can't get time to do it."

"You fly too?"

"Some small ones," he responded. She saw him glance at the clock in the kitchen and straightened in her seat.

"You need to head out?" she asked, checking the time for herself.

"In a minute. I have a little confession to make."

Her eyes narrowed on his face. "You mean you've been holding something back?"

"Yeah, well, I guess I haven't been very up front with you in the past. But I see where you're coming from, now. Monica had some mighty strange living arrangements and questionable bedmates. I don't think it's fair for you to go digging blind." He held up a hand when she might have commented. "I still don't think digging is a great idea either, especially alone, but I don't want you over your head."

"Are you talking about Tower, or Monica's other employer?" Camille waited for a reaction. She was disappointed when he merely nodded.

"Tower was just one of the men that she was involved with, although she led me to believe that her relationship with him had been over for several months."

"I thought you didn't know anything about him? Now you've changed your story? Was she in the habit of updating you on her love life?" Camille's voice was just slightly too sharp.

"If you're implying that we were involved," he returned stiffly, "then you're wrong. Monica tended toward men that could get her somewhere. That wasn't me." He didn't sound resentful so much as resigned. Camille wondered what that revealed about him.

"I'm not implying, but it's a valid question. Just because you're willing to talk doesn't necessarily mean that I'm getting the whole truth."

"So now I'm a suspect?" He looked curiously calm, and slightly amused.

"Shouldn't you be?"

"You're awfully comfortable here if you really think I had anything to do with Monica's death."

Camille felt her face heat and lifted her chin a notch. "I really am going on gut instinct," she responded slowly. "I just have this idea that

92

I'd know it if I met the murderer. Women's intuition, if you like."

"Man! You are naïve," he said, exasperated.

She was having a hard time being angry with his doubts. His comments echoed what she had heard multiple times from Leo, but it still rankled.

"I really doubt you know me well enough to make such a sweeping," she hesitated, searching for the right word and hitting a pointed one instead," moronic statement."

His face registered a flash of surprise before his habitual blank expression slid into place. "That's between you and you're therapist," he said bluntly, and held up one hand. "I just thought it was something of my duty, maybe not my best interest, to help you out a little."

She yanked a hand though her already rumpled hair and pulled her feet up beneath her in one fluid movement.

"Alright. Truce." She sighed and eased a kink from her neck. "You have an idea of who Monica might have pissed off."

"From my side of the wall, it was more like who didn't she? Almost all of her relationships ended in slammed doors and shouting. It was the results that I never saw. I don't know if she made up with these guys or just moved on."

"What's your gut instinct?"

"I think she held on."

Camille looked skeptical. She couldn't imagine that-stringing on two or more volatile relationships at one time. But something in Max's voice had her examining him more closely.

"What do you know?"

"I know that not a week before she died, Monica was looking for another apartment and sending out resumes. I also know she wasn't very concerned about money lately and got herself in something of a bind. She came to me for a loan."

"You?"

"A small loan. She asked and I couldn't say no."

Camille sat for a moment, her thoughts spinning. Monica wanted to move, wanted to change jobs, leave town perhaps.

"Do you think she was going to disappear?"

"I didn't think of it at the time, but now," his eyes narrowed slightly and he leaned forward, "now it makes some sense. It makes good

The Parrot Told Me

sense, don't you think?"

~*~

Camille was surprised at how long that Max stayed. After he had finished his coffee, he lingered, his expression serious.

"I don't know what to think about this situation, but I don't want you to get hurt. I can see why your friend Leo is worried. You look like you haven't slept any more than I have, and I can tell that you have trouble thinking of anything else."

It was on the tip of her tongue to admit the truth. She wanted to tell him about her history, about Darcy, and about the loss she had suffered. But she didn't want him to look at her the way Leo sometimes did. She didn't want the pity, she wanted him to believe her. In the end, she said nothing.

Chapter 10

By the next evening, Camille was still stalking around the apartment, restless and uneasy. Even Simon could feel her upset, and paced with her around the top of the cage, making disgruntled noises. She stopped to switch on the TV, only to turn it off almost immediately. Camille knew that she should feel better. Talking with Max had been nice. Perhaps she had gotten too worked up with her afternoon experience, but she just couldn't get settled.

She jumped when the phone rang. Unconsciously, she placed a hand against her stomach and froze. She closed sat on the kitchen chair slowly. Her hand trembled, ever so slightly, as she picked up the receiver.

"Camille."

It was her mother, but Camille had already known.

"Mom?"

"Cammy, I need you to come home."

"Now? Mom…"

"It's alright. Dad and I are fine. We just need to talk. We need to see you."

Camille ran a hand through her hair in a quick, frustrated gesture.

"Tell me, mom."

"Not over the phone." Her mother's voice changed and caught. "You come home as soon as you can," a deep sigh hid some emotion. "But Camille, it's not an emergency; it'll keep. You be careful."

~*~

When Leo arrived five minutes later, Camille was not surprised. His face was grim but controlled, and Camille couldn't help but feel some relief at his steady presence. What if her world were crumbling again?

"What do you know?" she snapped as she scooped up her long

The Parrot Told Me

rain coat.

"Nothing," he said, taking the coat from her chilly fingers and wrapping it around her shoulders.

"Leo, really…"

"Your mom asked me to come and get you, no more, no less." Camille was silent as she eased into the late model trans-am and buckled her belt. Her mind felt full, but her stomach an empty cavern. The buttery leather seat which had always given her a stab of envy seemed uncomfortably stiff.

"It must be something serious. Do you think one of them is sick? Oh, God, Leo, I couldn't stand for that. Or something to do with the rest of the family? Or Darcy?" she said at last, looking at Leo's rigid profile. "Leo, what if they've found something out about Darcy?"

"What are you thinking? Didn't they close the case years ago?"

"In a manner of speaking," Camille said softly, her hand going up to rub her eyes. "Almost three months after Darcy disappeared, a man was caught and convicted for the kidnapping of an eighteen year old college student at Eastern Kentucky University." Camille dropped her hands in her lap. "It was exactly the same circumstance as Darcy's disappearance. The only difference was that the girl escaped."

"Did they find any connection between the girls?"

Camille closed her eyes, a ripple of pain tracing behind her eyes.

"Yes, actually." Her smile was bitter. "They had both worked at the same ice cream shop that summer. When the man was questioned, he pretty much admitted to Darcy's kidnapping, but just not in so many words. Not enough to let us know the whole story, or what happened to her." She looked out the window blindly, seeing her own pale reflection. "There weren't enough deals in the system to persuade him to tell us where she was." Camille paused and let out a slow sigh. "Campbell Buff. Now that's a name I'll never forget. Or forgive."

"Let's not jump to any conclusions until we have a chance to see your parents." Leo's voice was soft, but firm.

They road in silence as the clouds gathered around the sun like vultures, finally drowning out the light. When they reached Camille's parents' home, a light cold mist was blanketing the car.

Camille was out of the car before Leo had turned off the rumbling motor. She jogged up the sidewalk, raced up the stairs, and burst through

96

the front door.

"Mom? Dad!"

Her parents walked together from the living room. Her mom had been crying, and her father as well, although he took more trouble to hide it.

Her mom folded her into her arms, into the familiar scent and warmth of childhood.

"It's Darcy, isn't it," Camille choked on the words.

"They've found her, Cammy." Her mother sighed and held Camille lightly by her arms as though unable to give up the physical contact.

"Where?" The question wasn't what Camille wanted to ask. She wanted to know if her sister was possibly, however impossible, alive. But she knew it wasn't true, and she couldn't bear to hurt her parents any more.

"In Versailles. Close." Her father put a heavy arm around Camille's shoulder. "A homeowner took down his shed in an adjacent field and pulled up the concrete slab. He found her grave."

~*~

Camille found out the details later. The dental records had been enough to identify the body, and the skull fracture had given them a probable cause of death. It would take time for the remains to be released, but Camille's parents wanted to look for burial plots as soon as possible. Camille wasn't sure she was ready for that.

Camille left with Leo, relieved that her parents hadn't wanted her company for that particular task. The mist had deepened into a lightly drifting rain, full of wet and chill. Camille didn't notice she was damp until she stood outside her apartment door and numbly watched the beads of moisture sink into her jacket.

Leo took Camille's keys and unlocked the door for her. When he stood aside, Camille hesitated at the doorway, an uneasy trickle chilling her spine.

She forced herself forward, hitting the wall switch and throwing the living room into soft illumination. A breath she hadn't realized she had been holding, escaped her lips in a sigh. How could it all look so

The Parrot Told Me

normal? How could everything look the same when her life definitely wasn't?

"You sure you don't want me to stay?" Leo closed the door behind them and prowled around the room, unconsciously shifting magazines and tossing pillows. His nervous energy seemed to vibrate the air around him.

"Yes, I'm sure," she responded quickly, wanting nothing more than quiet and calm.

He looked at her doubtfully.

"You have my number on speed dial?"

She sighed and nodded, putting her hands on her hips.

"I'm good, but thanks. If I need you, I'll call. I promise."

He stepped close to her and slipped a brotherly arm around her shoulders. The kiss her dropped on her forehead was brisk.

"Okay," he said, his voice slightly hoarse.

"Okay," she whispered back.

~*~

She wanted to play music, but she couldn't bear to hear any dialogues from the bird. She chose a sappy sentimental country ballad and settled down with wine and her regrets.

She knew she couldn't get drunk. She was afraid of her own dreams as much as her memories, and tomorrow might hold more than she could cope with.

She couldn't read. She couldn't concentrate. She put her glass back on the trunk and tucked her feet beneath her. Doubts crowded her mind. Why had she been so shocked about her sister? Did she really think that her death wasn't the inevitable conclusion?

She stood impatiently and paced to the window. Perhaps she had. Maybe it was a normal hope, if impractical, impossible, to think that her sister had escaped the killer and melted into some other life, safe but separate.

Her breath fogged the glass as she looked out into the April night. Winter was finally yielding to the warmth of spring. Ironic.

She put her fingertips to the glass and concentrated on her prints. When they were children, she and Darcy had made endless doodles on

98

car windows, bedroom windows, and their glass back door.

She hadn't realized she was crying until the damp hit her arm with a warm plop. The blurring made it easier. She pulled her hands back and crossed her arms protectively over her middle. Her breath was catching now in ugly hiccups.

The knock at the door made her turn slowly, shoulders slumped. She didn't bother wiping her face but stomped to the door, her eyes wide and wet.

"Leo," she said, pulling the door open.

She froze when she saw Max in the doorway, his big hands stuffed in his pockets. Her first impulse, to simply close the door, would have been the wisest one. She felt too brittle to fight, and her pale tear stained face held no secrets.

"I wanted to, that is, could you spare a minute?" He shifted awkwardly, his booted feet leaving deep prints in the carpet.

"Now is really not..."

He finally focused on her face, and she saw the concern rise in his eyes. "Are you alright? Did something happen?" One strong hand reached out to catch her shoulder.

"I just got some sad news," she said weakly.

"Can I come in?"

Without reason, she stepped aside and let him in.

Behind his back, she closed the door and used her sleeves to wipe at her damp cheeks. Her lips tasted of salt and her face felt hot and tight. She watched mutely as he dropped into a seat in her living room, leaving the battered couch to her.

She folded into the cushions like a paper doll, her arms crossed again over her chest. Ahh, if he would just disappear, if all of it would just disappear, just for a while. She looked longingly at the wine shimmering in the glass.

"What happened?" His voice was hushed and almost reverent. Without the obscuring beard or whiskers, he looked younger and somehow more approachable. His light eyes, intense on her face, looked concerned.

"I found out something," she responded slowly, the words dropping out of her mouth.

His only response was to scoot forward and continue the

The Parrot Told Me

examination of her face as though the reasons could be read in her eyes.

"They found my sister's body today." She stopped, horrified at the what she had said, shattered at what the words meant.

She felt rather than heard his sudden intake of breath. "She's been gone for such a long time, but..." she breathed, her head dropping. She heard the words but never remembered forming them. "She left home one evening end never came back." The story slipped out while Camille seemed to view it all at a distance. She could almost see herself, a much younger self, curled up in the hallway while the police spoke to her mother. Gone. Her sister was gone and now never to return.

When the story was done and her words had dried up, Camille sat with her hands clasped in her lap, hot tear drops soaking into the sleeve of her shirt.

"Camille," Max said softly and she could see his outline shift.

"Damn," she muttered into her hands. "I don't mean to. I can't stop," she stuttered, the sobs breaking up her words.

"Don't then." His voice was soft, deep. "Cry as much as you need to." She felt rather than saw him move beside her and his weight on the cushion shifted her towards him. The arm he dropped around her shoulder was heavy, but his shirt was soft and he smelled surprisingly good, soap and skin.

She cried for a timeless moment, first sitting stiffly against the warmth of his chest, but gradually leaning in, letting him rock her like a child. For a moment she shed her mask and let herself take the comfort that she desperately needed. Her grief eventually faded and she took a deep breath before wiping her face with an already damp tissue and giving her nose a mighty blow. When she straightened, Max immediately backed away to give her a moment.

"I'll be back," she said, and stood quickly, almost tripping on her shoes she had carelessly tossed off. She kicked them out of the way, a trifle too forcefully, and bolted from the room without looking back. She didn't want to see his expression; she didn't want to know what he thought of her. She slipped into the bathroom and stopped in front of the mirror. With shaking hands, she grabbed a flowered washcloth off the rack. She wet it with cool water and applied it to her face, silently cursing her own weakness. She didn't need to do this now. She needed to hold it together for just a little bit longer. She would find out what Max needed, and then shove him out the door.

She looked back at her reflection. Pale, yes, and red eyed. Her nose was definitely pink, her face pinched. She looked older, and realized that her innocence had somehow been tested again. Again. It was like living through those hours again. You would think it would be easier the second time. It wasn't.

~*~

When she returned to the room, she did so without apology. It was already awkward enough without trying to justify her natural emotions. Instead, she took her seat and faced him, composed at least on the outside.

She caught him, for a moment, unaware. He looked older too, and tired, with fine lines tracing his eyes and forehead. His dark eyes were unfocused; his gaze caught by the flickering candlelight or perhaps his own thoughts. He certainly wasn't the threat that she had first thought him to be.

"You said you were going to work?"

He looked up quickly, his gaze clearing as though the thoughts were never there. "Yes, but what I wanted to talk about wasn't that important. Mara just gave me a call and gave me another warning for you. But just now, it doesn't seem that dire."

"Thanks, anyway," she said weakly, and leaned back into the soft cushion of the couch.

"Look, I'll come by later and we can talk. I think you need to rest just now."

She nodded mutely and watched him stand. She couldn't summon the strength to go with him to the door, but sat watching him from the couch. He ran his hand over his hair and looked at her gravely. Without speaking, he bent and dropped a kiss on her forehead.

"You have my number. You call me if you need anything."

Her eyes followed him to the apartment door and she watched with wry amusement as he locked the door knob and pulled it closed behind him. When the sound of his footsteps retreated, she pulled the throw from the back of the couch and wrapped it around her shoulders, huddling down for warmth that wasn't likely to come.

The Parrot Told Me

When she fell asleep, her mind was on Monica, but her dreams were Darcy's.

Chapter 11

Darcy's funeral. Oh, God, had she ever though that it would happen? Her breath caught in half prayer. She would need all of the spiritual help she could get on this day. Somehow, before, she had talked herself into a separate, Darcy free, life. In high school, she had rebelled in a million different ways. She chopped and colored her hair, pierced ears and navel, and set out to make herself as different from her brainy, mainstream sister as possible. College had been a struggle, a degree earned in starts and stops with a dozen jobs between. She had dressed and styled and molded herself into something else, someone who didn't resemble Darcy in the telling glass of the mirror.

Camille dropped her disguise for the funeral, opting to wear tailored black clothes and softly styled hair. She wore one pair of earrings and one single pearl ring. Her black flats hadn't been worn for years, perhaps since the last funeral.

In the mirror, she looked all too familiar. She sighed and turned away from the glass. She wondered how Darcy would have aged had she made it to thirty, how the lines would have sketched their experiences in her ever youthful visage.

The bell was ringing; Leo had come for her. Visitation had seemed too much for Camille's family, so they had settled for a small ceremony in their parish of St. John's.

Leo planned to drive her car. The sports car just didn't seem appropriate. Camille was grateful for his sensitivity. He had always managed to somehow know just what she needed, even if she was a little confused about it herself.

She sighed and added a bit of blush to her cheeks. Leo would scold if she looked too pale. A strange type of mother hen, that was for sure, but he had settled seamlessly into the role. Her female friends often asked why she hadn't pressed the relationship into something more. It wasn't as though Leo was unattractive, or their compatibility was in

The Parrot Told Me

question. But it just wasn't right. The romantic feelings didn't exist, and she valued their relationship too much to try to make it into something it wasn't.

With a sigh, she opened her apartment door and let him step in, their greeting wordless. He gave her a quick, firm embrace and walked past her into the kitchen. While she gathered her purse and coat, she listened for movements in the kitchen. When he returned, she saw that he carried a few water bottles and a full box of Kleenex.

"Ready to go?"

She smiled sadly and hooked her arm through his. "I'm as ready as I can be," she said softly and pulled the door closed.

~*~

She would never remember the funeral in any detail. It was a blur of faces, solemn expressions, stiff poses, and the scent of flowers. The casket was a shiny rose colored box, far too large for the remains tucked within. There were copious flowers, baskets bursting with ivy and mums, baby's breath cradling bouquets of roses, and mixed blossom arrangements in plastic containers to be taken to the gravesite. The familiar church was oddly comforting. Camille had rejected religion for her teen years, but gradually developed a cautious agreement with God, she wouldn't get in His way if He didn't get in hers. It pained her mother, and she knew that her religious parents harbored a deep hope that she would one day return to her Catholic roots. She knelt at the front of the church and gazed at the windows until the colors blurred into a single brilliant, multifaceted jewel. She felt at home in the snug arms of the church, but wasn't sure if she was ready to forgive God for the unforgivable. Letting her lose her sister.

Leo stood at the gravesite, his pale faced set and dry eyed. He had held her elbow, handed her tissues, and guided her through the ceremony when she couldn't even recall her own name. As the last goodbyes were said, Camille finally raised her head to look at the other mourners. There were her parents' old friends, familiar faces from the parish, a few lightly lined faces from Darcy's own class, and a flock of strangers, cameras pointed and avid eyes seeking the sensationalism of a long ago tragedy. Apparently some of the media hadn't forgotten, and were resurrecting the brutal past to show on the nightly news.

Camille felt faintly ill and looked away. She had forgotten that part of the tragedy so many years ago, but seeing those cameras made it fresh again. The ache was overwhelming, and she felt herself bend toward her mother. For their part, her parents looked pale and dignified. Their eyes were damp, and Camille could tell that they hadn't had enough sleep for some time, but they were strong. She let her mother draw her into a hug and breathed in the familiar scent. Over her mother's shoulder she could see a few more figures standing at a distance. Some of her workers from the bookstore were clustered in the shade of an ancient oak tree, and standing alone in the sunlight was Max, his dark hair blowing softly, his head lowered as though in prayer.

~*~

Camille was back at work the next day, feeling stiff and tired, as though getting over a prolonged illness. Her mother would be coming later to go to lunch with her, and Leo was keeping a close eye on her. But over all, she felt better than she had anticipated. She had known her sister was gone; it just took the ceremony to close the book on her young life.

She worked on simple chores, unboxing and shelving books, polishing windows, and cleaning out the coffee pot so that she wouldn't have to deal with customers. The case of her sister's kidnapping was locally known enough that there were some well-meaning people who still wanted to express their sympathy. It was too new for that. Camille assured Leo that she just needed some time, so she hid among her beloved books.

After lunch with her mother, Camille decided that she wanted to go back home instead of finishing the day. She was so tired, and her body and mind ached for a few minutes of oblivion. She avoided looking at anyone in the lobby of the apartment building, and left her mailbox unemptied. She unlocked her door quickly and quietly, and slipped inside. She had kicked off her shoes and was putting on a pot of coffee when the bell rang. Frowning, she went to the door and tiptoed to peer out the peep hole. She hadn't seen Max since the cemetery, and she knew that Leo was at the shop working. She was puzzled to see an unfamiliar

The Parrot Told Me

figure outside the door.

It was a woman, thin to the point of looking unhealthy, with a sallow complexion and grim expression. She looked sad, but not alarming, so Camille opened the door.

"Yes?" she said, holding the door only slightly open.

"Are you Camille?" The woman asked, her voice soft and southern, drawing out the sounds like music. The cadence was familiar. She knew immediately that this woman's presence had something to do with Monica.

"Yes, I am."

The woman looked relieved, her lined face softening slightly. "You were a friend of my cousin Monica?"

Friend might have been an exaggeration, but the woman's expression looked so hopeful, Camille couldn't say otherwise.

"Right, and you're Monica's cousin?"

"Oh, yes. My name is Danni, Danielle Wise? Monica probably mentioned me. Her family lived with mine when she was just 12 or so, that was when her daddy fell on hard times. I was a little older than she was, but she followed me everywhere." The woman's face became solemn, as though recalling why she was there. "She was such a sweet little thing," she murmured, her eyes fixed on what Camille could only assume was a picture of a younger and gentler Monica that had settled in the other woman's memory.

Camille wasn't sure what to say. Tell the woman that no, she had never heard a story about Monica's childhood? Tell her Monica never spoke of any family? Tell her that Monica really only had one friend that she could count on, and that friend was trying to block any chance at finding out what had happened to Monica?

Instead, she opened the door slowly and forced a smile. "Monica didn't tell me too much about her family, but I am glad to meet you. Is there something I can do for you?"

The woman smiled and looked so relieved that Camille felt guilty. "Well, I came up here to pack up poor Monica's belongings. We just got news a week ago that we needed to clear her apartment out. I was the only one who could come. Our Gramma is getting on in years, but I wanted to bring some of Monica's things home to her." She paused, looking pained at the idea of Monica's possessions. "I was hoping that some of Monica's friends might help me go through her things, and in her last letter, she mentioned you by name."

Camille was surprised. Why had Monica mentioned her name? Surely Monica's closest friend was Mara? She would be better to go through the dead woman's things than Camille. But Danni looked so earnest, that Camille found herself nodding. "I, uh, I'll do what I can." She watched the emotions pass over the other woman's face and sighed. She had her own baggage to deal with, and now this.

"That would just be great. I'm staying at a hotel a few blocks over and thought we could get started on Saturday or Sunday. Will you be off work then?"

"Saturday will be fine," Camille said slowly, feeling as though her brain wasn't processing at normal speed. She could think of no reason to refuse Danni, and although she still felt the weight of her sister's death, she knew that Monica's cousin was feeling pain as well. She could see it in her eyes, and her grateful look for the promised help. Almost as though she read Camille's hesitation, Danni smiled shyly and started backing away.

"I'll see you on Saturday then? Around ten okay for you?"

Camille nodded and watched the thin figure retreat back down the hall. Her chest felt tight, and she found that her hands were clenched around the doorjamb. She didn't want to go back to Monica's apartment. With Darcy's funeral, Camille had come to the realization that she was getting in over her head with her attempts at investigation. She knew that something had happened to Monica, but how had it become her job to solve this particular crime? She really needed to concentrate on getting her own life back on track. She could see now that many of her adult decisions, and her issues with relationships, were most likely related to her sister's disappearance.

As she closed the door, she made a promise to herself. Helping Danni with Monica's belongings would be her last act as amateur sleuth. She would help pack away Monica's things, and with that symbolic act, close out that part of her own life.

~*~

The Parrot Told Me

She called her mother to check up the next evening after work. Her father would be taking the rest of the week off, and her mother said they were thinking about a little vacation.

"You would be welcome to come along," her mother assured her. "We were thinking about going to Florida. We haven't been there for a while, and the warm weather always makes your father feel better."

Camille made her excuses, but felt a little stab of sweet regret. Her parents were trying to move on, and the idea of a trip seemed like a good one to her. Maybe she would follow their example later and go on a little vacation herself. But for now, she still had some things to do.

"Mom, I wanted to ask your opinion of something," she said, trying to force her voice to sound light. She had told her mom only of the death of her neighbor, and about Simon and his various talents. She had deliberately left out any of her suspicions about Monica's death, trying to shield her parents from any unnecessary worry. Now she told her briefly about Danni's request.

"I don't really want to go up there and clear out Monica's things. I didn't really know her well at all. But I feel like her cousin really needs someone to help."

Camille's mother interrupted. "I think you need to help her. Think about how many people have helped us to deal with Darcy's death, both back then and now. It sounds like this lady needs some help, and she hasn't anyone else to turn to."

Camille smiled sadly. Her mother was giving her the best advice, of course, and even if it wasn't what she wanted to do, it was doing what was right. She sighed and laid out her clothes for the next day, work jeans and a tee shirt, casual and perfect for a day of walking through someone else's memories.

~*~

Danni showed up precisely on time, dressed reasonably in jeans and a tee shirt bearing the logo of Fort Myers beach. Camille wondered if she wore it in reflection of some old memories of family vacations. Almost as though Danni could hear her thoughts, Danni smiled wryly and pointed to her chest.

"Monica and I went with my folks when we were teenagers. I

thought it might give me a good memory to concentrate on." Danni stood outside in the hallway, and glanced down the length. "Quiet around here, isn't it?"

Camille nodded and pulled her apartment door closed behind her. "Most of the residents here are out of the building on Saturdays. The weekends are either really loud, or really empty. But Mrs. Patterson doesn't tolerate much out of anyone."

Danni nodded and followed after Camille as she led the way up the stairs. The hallway was quiet, the carpet muffling their steps. All the lights were lit, but it still seemed dim. Camille shivered and looked down the hall behind them. She felt eyes on her back, and wished she had Leo with her, or Max. Someone who was big and strong and worried about her health.

Danni had the key to Monica's apartment tucked in her pocket, and they stopped for a moment while she dug it out. It was quiet. Camille hadn't thought about it, but what she had told Danni was true. Mrs. Patterson didn't allow much noise. In fact, the loudest person in the complex had been Monica. In retrospect, it was curious that Mrs. Patterson had tolerated Monica's questionable behavior.

With that thought lingering, Camille followed Danni into the apartment. Danni must have been in earlier; there was a pile of broken down cardboard boxes in the center of the living room with a roll of tape balanced on top. Garbage bags, rubber gloves, and other cleaning supplies were tucked into two large buckets.

"Okay, so where do you want to start?" Danni looked overwhelmed. She stood in the doorway, her eyes scanning the accumulated memories of a woman recently deceased.

Camille stood next to her and rubbed her hands through her cropped hair. What was she doing here? Didn't she have enough grief? Did she have to add to it by cleaning up after another tragedy?

She turned to Danni, words on her lips, ready to beg off the job. But she couldn't. Danni stood in silence, tears coursing down her thin face. She wiped her checks with the heel of her hand, turning away slightly. Her worn face reminded Camille of what it had felt like when she had first lost her sister. The unreality of the absence, the loss of the person, and the loss of the childhood memories that went with them. Losing Monica must have been a little like that for Danni. Even if they

The Parrot Told Me

hadn't been as close as adults, it was evident that Danni still felt that Monica was family, and that Danni still held fast to those childhood ties.

"I will start in her bedroom and bathroom," Camille said gently. "They might be harder for you." She leaned over and gathered a few bags and a small stack of boxes. "What do you want to take home? Do you want to keep her clothes, or give some away to charity?"

Danni gave her a wry smile, wiping her face with a brisk gesture. "Do I look like I'm going to fit in any of her things? Monica was always more curvy than me. Just put things in boxes, and I'll take them to our church." She gathered some boxes and looked up at Camille. "If you find anything you want to keep, feel free."

Camille nodded and went into the bedroom, her face set. There was nothing of Monica's that she wanted, and the memories that clung to the place made her shiver. She was glad that Danni was going to take the things to charity. Monica's wardrobe might have been a little eccentric, but some of the pieces would be really nice for someone in need. And Camille knew that she would feel better when Monica's things were gone and the sad story would finally be over.

In the bedroom, she looked around slowly and tried to decide where to start. The bathroom door stood open, and after a moment, Camille decided that it would be best to a get it over with. She took the boxes and bags into the room and started to go through the dead woman's

Things. After about an hour, toiletries and paper products were tossed in a garbage bag, the towels neatly folded in one of the boxes, and the candles, both burnt and not, dropped on top of the trash. Just touching them made Camille feel faintly ill. When she had cleared out the cabinet and the rest of the debris, she went out to get the cleaning supplies from the living room. She could hear Danni in the kitchen, the gentle clink of glassware and rattle of silverware as she shifted and packed things away. Camille didn't disturb the other woman. She wanted to be done, and was feeling a little too vulnerable. If she started talking about Monica, she was afraid it would be here sister's face she would see, and that was something she knew she couldn't cope with just now.

She wiped up the bathroom with paper towels and cleaner, noting mostly dust from the empty apartment. The bathtub had already been scrubbed clean, and Camille didn't even want to have to think about whose chore that had been. After a final wipe down of the floor, Camille looked back at the room, satisfied that it was clean and ready for the next tenant. She suspected that it would be recleaned by someone that Mrs. Patterson hired, but she knew that Danni would not like leaving the apartment in less than spotless condition.

In the bedroom, she bundled the sheets, blankets, and other linens and dropped them in a laundry basket Monica had kept in her spacious walk in closet. The things in the basket really needed to be washed, and since each apartment had hookups for their own washer and dryer, it would be easy enough to wash them before they were packed away. Camille doubted that anyone in Danni's family would have use for Monica's rather exotic looking decorations, but someone else might. She took dragged the basket out of the closet and began to gather clothes from the floor. She was glad that this hadn't been Danni's job. There was something faintly embarrassing looking at another person's underwear, especially when it was as unusual as Monica's. Most of it Camille stuffed in a second garbage bag to be disposed of later.

Once the bed was stripped, she started on the nightstand and dresser, steadily packing up books and photos while taking more questionable items and dropping them in the trash. Letters and other correspondence was sparse, and Camille figured she must have kept most of that in another room. But, with the digital age, perhaps there wasn't as much of a paper trail that hinted at someone's life and loves.

The closet was last. She pulled items off hangers and folded them into boxes, carefully stacking the nicer coats and jackets on the top. Shoes were plentiful and still in their respective boxes. These Camille stacked outside the closet door to look through later. On the top shelves were odds and ends that Monica had collected. A small collection of stuffed bears, a few baby dresses, and some old grade school papers were packed away in a box on one shelf. It was obvious that these were some favorites that Monica had kept from her childhood. Camille took the box and laid it outside the closet as well to let Danni see the contents. She hoped that they would bring back some sweet memories for Monica's grieving cousin.

When the closet was empty, she went through and dusted the shelves and cleaned out the last of the hangers. When she was done, she went into the living area where Danni had left Monica's vacuum sitting in the middle of the floor. Since Camille could still hear Danni working

The Parrot Told Me

in the kitchen, she pulled the vacuum into the bedroom and cleaned the floors in the closet.

The bedroom looked strangely empty now. Camille took down the few pictures from the walls, and left the furniture as it was. It would be up to Danni to decide what to do with the larger pieces. She would need a moving truck to empty the whole apartment. The many boxes of shoes and the box of childhood things were all that remained. Camille took the box of Monica's treasured items, and carried it into the living room. Danni was standing there, her thin face already looking tired.

"I found these in the closet. I thought they might be some things that you would remember. You don't have to deal with them now."

When Camille put the box on the floor, Danni approached it and gingerly opened the top.

"Oh, I remember this!" she said, her voice soft and amazed. "Our Monica loved bears and had a huge collection of them. Most of them were second hand, but she didn't care one bit." She sighed and hugged one to her chest. "She even has some of the little dresses her mama got her. She loved to dress up when she was young." She carefully pulled out a small stack of letters clipped together with a plastic chip clip from a local grocery store. "Ha, and these are from me! I sent her letters when she first moved away from home." She held the letters like they were treasured documents of the past and sighed again. "I'm so glad she kept them. It means she knew we were thinking of her." She looked up at Camille, her faded blue eyes shining with tears, "You do think she remembered we loved her, don't you?"

Camille felt the hard pull in her chest as pictures of her vivacious neighbor blended with those of her teenaged sister, both lost too young. "Yes, I think she knew she was loved."

Danni carefully placed the things back in the box and dug around in her pocket for a tissue. "Well, I'm starting to get hungry. Why don't you let me buy you a burger?"

Camille could see that she wanted to get out of the apartment, and she didn't blame her at all. But she knew that there was still a lot of work to do, and really didn't want to come back a second day. "Would you mind getting something and bringing it back? I can do a little more work and then we can eat together."

Danni nodded slowly. "If that's what you want."

112

Rachael Rawlings

"It will be fine. There is a great burger place about a block away. I'll give you directions. Maybe we can even have a milk shake." Camille forced a smile and led the other woman to the door. "I'll go through a few more things, and we can get going on the living room next."

After getting directions and Camille's order, Danni left by herself, and Camille closed the door after her. She stood with her hands on her hips, surveying the small apartment. It was already looking sad and empty. She went to the stack of shoe boxes and flipped open the lid. Inside was a pair of shiny black high heeled pumps, the toes pinched to an uncomfortable point. There were fairly plain, and although formal, they would be good for someone dressing up for a night out. But the boxes would take up far too much room if Danni were going to pack all of the items up together to go to charity. Camille went to the kitchen and pulled out a handful of small plastic bags that she had seen on her first visit to the apartment. She bagged the first pair of shoes and packed them into a box, hopeful that the plastic would help keep the shoes in better condition. The next box held gold heels, dotted with rhinestones. In the next two boxes, Camille found some practical running shoes. She noticed that each box still was stuffed with the protective paper, and when she reached into the running shoes, she saw that the toes were still stuffed with paper. Apparently Monica had really liked her shoes. The next box held more heels, and when Camille dug the paper out of the toes, there was something hard inside. She unrolled the paper, thinking she might have found some secret that Monica had hidden, only to find a doll's head, its stiff china face grimacing with unshed tears, not much bigger than a golf ball. The hair was stiff and golden, clinging to the scalp in a slick ponytail that was held in place by a miniature blue ribbon. Her lips were painted a rosy pink, and her cold cheeks had a faint blush. But her eyes were a wide, staring blue, and Camille shivered. She put the head aside with distaste, and went on to the next pair of shoes. Among the stacks were knee high boots, hot pink heels almost too high to be worn, strappy sandals with silver buckles, a variety of flat ballet type shoes probably for work, and more boots for nasty weather. Weirdly enough, there were also more dolls heads. There were two brunettes with pinched lips and brown eyes, another blond, and a baby head bald but for a twist of ceramic hair. None of the heads were larger than the first, and all had been stuffed into the toe of one of the shoes. Camille put the heads aside

The Parrot Told Me

and packed up the shoes in the plastic bags to be boxed. The shoes would hopefully find a good home. She looked at the small pile of heads and bundled them into one of the plastic bags. It was a strange collection, and she was hesitant to let Danni see them. There was something disturbing about the disembodied heads.

When Danni returned with their meal, she seemed to have once again regained her composure. She dropped the food on the table and smiled at Camille. "I can't tell you how much I appreciate all your help. I don't think I could have done this by myself."

Camille nodded, and unwrapped her burger, the smell of the food making her realize how hungry she was. "I don't mind helping. I lost my sister when I was younger, and I remember so many people helping us at the time. I can't imagine having to go through something like this alone."

Danni nodded. "Monica and I were so close when we were younger. When Monica got older, she couldn't wait to get out of town. She went to New York for a while to try to sell her art, but she said she couldn't make it there. When she settled here, we were really happy. We figured that she would find some friends, maybe get married, settle down." Danni took a thoughtful bite of her own burger. Her eyes skimmed the little room, looking at the different pieces of Monica's art lining the walls. "She just wanted to paint." Her voice was sad again, regretful.

"She had a show set up for her paintings," Camille said slowly, looking around at the number of works surrounding them. "We found out that from a neighbor. Maybe you could call the studio and have the showing for her."

Danni looked surprised. "I didn't know," she said, her voice soft. "Last time I heard from Monica, she said she had some news, but she wouldn't say what. She was going to come home to see the family in a few weeks. I bet she was going to tell us about the show." Her eyes filled as she took in a ragged breath. "Why couldn't she have lived to see that show?"

Camille felt her heart turn over as she looked at the other woman's grief. "We can call the studio today. We can at least see if they would be willing to keep the show date." Camille paused, "But only if you would want to go through with the show."

Danni looked at the painting propped up on the easel and nodded. "All of this just goes back to the family. It would be better for Monica's memory if we at least tried to get it in a show. It's what she wanted."

Camille nodded. "I'll find the number and we can call them on Monday. How long will you be in town?"

Danni looked at the accumulated things in the living room, the piles of boxes and bags. "I don't know exactly, but I have a week off from work. Surely that will be enough time to get this taken care of?"

Camille smiled, her face sympathetic. "It should give us plenty of time," she said, gathering up her garbage. "We will get as much done today as we can, and then decide how much longer we will need to work."

~*~

By the end of the day, Camille was feeling grungy and tired, despite how orderly most of Monica's things had been kept. She rubbed her neck and stretched, trying to shake out the kinks that all the bending had caused in her back muscles. Danni looked a little gray around the lips, and Camille worried that the packing had been too hard on her. She told her firmly to go home and assured her that she would close down and lock the apartment door. Danni nodded gratefully, admitting that she had a headache and wanted nothing more than to lie down. Almost as soon as Danni had gone, Camille went through the empty apartment and shut off lights. The place felt more empty and abandoned now, but without the personal items, it wasn't as eerie. There was a knock on Monica's door, and Camille startled. She slowly turned off the kitchen light and went to the door. In the dim light of the hallway, she could see Max, standing back from the door, his face tight and worried.

She pulled open the door and stepped back, allowing him to come in but leaving the door open behind him. She wanted to be here no longer than she needed to be.

"What are you doing in here?" he asked, harshly, surprised to see her.

"I'm helping Monica's cousin to pack up her things. She asked me to help."

Max's expression registered his surprise. "How do you know

The Parrot Told Me

Monica's cousin?"

"I don't really. It's a long story." Camille looked into the empty dimly lit room and sighed. She walked into the living area and stood beside the empty table that had once held the dying flowers, polished now and waiting to be moved out. Her bones felt weary. "Monica's cousin had no one else to turn to and nowhere else to go. I agreed to help her. She's a nice lady who has a big job in front of her, and a lot of good memories of Monica. That was nice to see. Someone will miss Monica." Her voice melted away and she shook her head. "Do you want something to drink? Coffee or something? I'm ready to get out of here."

Max's expression eased and he stepped back out of the apartment. "Come on. You need a break."

She walked out with him, locking the knob as she pulled the door closed. Max took her hand loosely in his, his fingers warm.

Chapter 12

Camille could feel herself relax as they opened the door to her apartment, the soft scent of spices and vanilla acting as a balm on her nerves. After Max moved past her, she closed the door and automatically locked it. For the hundredth time she wondered if she would ever feel the same about living here.

"I'll get us something to drink. I don't have many choices."

Max smiled slowly following her into the kitchen. "Coffee is fine. Why don't you let me help fix the coffee? You look dead on your feet."

In comfortable silence, she filled the pot with water and dumped it into the coffee maker. She measured out the coffee grounds, too tired to grind her own coffee, but added extra to make the brew stronger. Max got out the heavy mugs from the cabinet, and set out spoons and the sugar bowl. He went into the refrigerator to get out the creamer and laid them on the table in a neat array.

"Now sit down for a minute. Tell me about your week. I know that it must have been hell to live through, and I was worried when I didn't hear anything from you."

Camille moved to put away the stack of crisp white filters for the coffee maker, keeping her hands busy and her mind blank. She was glad that he couldn't see her face. The feelings were still too raw. She switched on the coffee maker and folded and refolded the hand towel by the sink.

"I'd really rather not talk about me," she said slowly, taking her chair across from his. "Why not change the topic for once and talk about you?"

"Not much to say." He shrugged looked out the lightly frosted window. "My sister is coming in next week. It's just the two of us in my family. She's bringing my niece and nephew. I promised a trip to the zoo." His face eased and he looked younger, softer. His eyes strayed to the coffee maker and then back to Camille. "Maybe you'd like to come?

The Parrot Told Me

My niece is five and really has a thing for the monkeys. I'm worried she's starting to act like one. My nephew thinks that the elephants are the best and wants to have one when he grows up. He's seven. I don't want to burst his bubble yet, but he's pretty sure next year is the year Santa will come through for him."

Camille was tempted to say no immediately. She couldn't imagine herself in that familial role. She couldn't picture a niece and nephew with sticky hands and adoring eyes. It had all disappeared with Darcy's death. But in truth, the day spent with children, acting like children, had appeal. Perhaps helping pack Monica's things was good in one way, but forgetting the situation for a day might be good for her as well.

In the end, she agreed to go. It was a date of sorts with a man she didn't know at all well, but who was getting more appealing with time. He wasn't polish perfect, but he was solid and direct and she felt somehow safe with him. She couldn't say how she knew, but she was certain that he cared for her as well.

After their coffee, he led her into the living area where she collapsed on the couch. She felt sleepy and momentarily content. He sat in the overstuffed chair and she turned on the TV. And let it play in the background. He filled the time with amusing stories of his adventures with his niece and nephew, making her picture how it would be to have that close bond, but without the ache that usually came with that idea. When he left, she felt a comfortable warmth that she hadn't felt for quite a while. She took a long hot shower, and mentally erasing the picture of Monica's bathroom so similar to hers, pulled on sweats and finger combed her hair in the mirror. When she was done, she checked the door for the locks and switched off all but the dimmest lights. She slept for ten hours that night, a deep, dreamless sleep.

Leo was at work on Thursday, looking like his perfect self. As though he could read her mood, he didn't bring up Monica or Camille's sister, and instead kept the conversation light. He was dating a new girl who was coming in for lunch. Camille felt an amused warmth in her heart when she realized that the introduction was Leo's version of introducing the girl to his family. For the confirmed bachelor that he was, it was a step for him to bring a girl here, much less to have her meet Camille.

~*~

In the few days that Camille hadn't seen Danni, she had to admit that Danni had never been far off her mind. The occasional bustle and settle of the apartment made Camille wonder if that could be Danni loading up yet another box of Monica's past into her car to be taken home, donated, or tossed. With the relative calm, Camille spent some time with her parents, struggling to put her own past together. She had taken Leo out for one visit and after dinner they had sat around the table, dropping an occasional story about Darcy. For Leo, the stories were all new, like a page from Camille's diary that had always remained shut for him. Camille found herself enjoying the bitter sweet memories and even asked for a picture of Darcy to take back to her apartment with her. She doubted she was ready to display it for all to see, but at least she would have it when she was ready for that step.

By the weekend, Camille was wondering if Danni had actually finished the task of packing up Monica's things and had finally headed home. Twice she had seen Chloe in the hall, looking as though she were just waiting for Camille to come in. Whether she wanted to ask about Leo, possible, or to discuss Monica and Danni, equally probable, Camille chose a different route to her apartment to avoid the discussion.

With Saturday morning came rain. It was a heavy, splashing rain that plopped in huge drops against the windows, running like rivulets of syrup down the panes. Max called to say that his sister had put off the trip until the weather would cooperate, and Camille felt a sharp surge of disappointment. After her initial hesitation about being with the children, she had checked her attitude, instead concentrating on the childish joy of cotton candy, miniature train rides, and the wonder of a child gazing at creatures so diverse and grand. A day with careless giggles and children's curiosity would have done her good. Now she sat in her too warm apartment, gazing at the same gray garden that was showcased from Monica's window above, and pondering what to do on her day off.

When the phone rang, she felt her heart stutter in alarm and rose quickly to answer it. Before her fingers could close around the receiver, Simon gave a very human "Hello?" and started his own conversation, silences punctuated by "yes, okay, okay, hum." Camille had heard this performance before and had found it funny. The fact that the voice was

119

The Parrot Told Me

neutral, neither the mystery man's nor Monica's familiar drawl, made it a little more comfortable. Camille echoed Simon's "Hello," and felt a silly since of joy when she heard Max's voice.

"Hey, I didn't know if you had made plans since I called this morning?" His voice was a deliberate casual, false, but a good attempt.

"No, not really. I was watching the rain."

"Okay," Simon said clearly in the background, "Love you, bye."

Camille chuckled and told Max, "Simon says he loves you."

Max laughed. "I didn't know I had made such a good impression."

"He loves everyone on the phone," Camille replied, grinning. It felt good, this silly banter.

"Well nice, since he's not so friendly in person. Listen, if you didn't have anything planned, I was wondering if you wanted to get some lunch. I saw Danni this morning, and she was asking if we would help with the final packing in the apartment tomorrow, so I thought we might try to get away today."

"You've been talking to Danni?"

"I met her outside of the apartment. She's been in almost every day. She's gotten the place in great shape. The moving trucks are due in the morning at 10 and I think she will be heading home after that." Max paused thoughtfully. "I think most of the things she is taking are for her grandmother, but she's already hauled out a few loads for charity."

Camille felt her happy mood fade. The last day of packing, moving Monica out. "I'd be happy to help Danni tomorrow. And yes, I think I'd like to get out today to do something fun."

She could almost hear the smile in Max's voice when he agreed to come down to her apartment in thirty minutes to take her out. They had no plans about what they might do, but it didn't feel like they needed any.

When Camille opened the door for Max, she was surprised to see that he was clean shaven, minus the glasses, and dressed neatly in jeans and a polo shirt. Under all the hair, he was quite a nice looking man. He wasn't the perfection that Leo had attained, but a rugged, comfortable handsome with big hands and blunt features. His eyes, the soft green of spring, were at odds with his dark hair and brows. She wondered why he would cover up his attractive face, but on second thought, realized that

120

it wasn't even something he was likely to think about. With a smile, she opened the door wide and let him step in.

"You look better," he said, with a bluntness of someone used to expressing their mind.

"Thank you, I think," she replied, closing the door behind him.

"Sorry, that came out wrong. You look better than the last time I saw you. How are you feeling?"

"Fine," she said, her tone light. "I have a few days off, and when this rain stops, I'm planning on going to pick out some spring flowers for my window boxes. I'm ready for the winter to be over."

He nodded in agreement and dropped into the couch, the soft cushions enveloping him. "Nice couch. I could sleep on this thing."

"It is comfortable," she agreed, sitting on edge. "How's Danni doing?"

"She seems to be fine. Nice lady. She had some boxes that you had packed, and she wasn't sure where they would go. You can help her label them tomorrow, and we'll try to get the furniture out. It looked like all the small things were packed away."

Camille nodded. "We did that earlier in the week. She did the kitchen while I did the bath and bedroom. We both did some in the living room, but I imagine that's what she has spent most of today doing." Camille looked down at her hands, her nails embarrassingly short and brittle from her manual labor. "There were some things I just didn't know what to do with."

"I'm sure you did your best. Danni can always get rid of some things that she doesn't want once she gets home."

"Yeah," Camille said softly, "but there were a few things I didn't know if I should just pitch."

"Like what?" max looked curious, but not intensely, just relaxed and comfortable.

"Well, I tossed most of the open toiletries, medicine, that kind of thing. And underwear." Camille bit her lip and glanced down to her hands. "She had some strange things too. She had all these shoes packed in boxes. I took them out of the boxes because they took too much space. In some of the shoes were, well the heads popped off of china dolls." Camille couldn't help but make a face. She hated china dolls that were whole and perfect, the disembodied heads were just plain awful.

The Parrot Told Me

"She had dolls heads in her shoes? Why?"

Camille shrugged. "I had thought maybe to protect the china when they were moved. They were wrapped in tissue paper and jammed in the toes of the shoes."

"That is just weird," Max said, sitting up a little straighter. "Dolls are for kids, and I really didn't see Monica with any kids."

"They can also be collector's items," Camille said slowly. "You know who collects them…"

"Mrs. Patterson. Been there. Talk about weird."

Camille nodded again and told him about her going in to sign the rental agreement. "I'm pretty sure Simon didn't like them either because he was really spooked the day that I moved him out."

"You think the heads could have been Mrs. Patterson's?" Max asked thoughtfully. He leaned forward, elbows on knees, and looked lost in thought. "Maybe Monica got mad at Mrs. Patterson and swiped some dolls from her apartment."

"They were just heads, not dolls, and I didn't see any dolls with no heads at Mrs. Patterson's apartment," Camille commented. "I see how they would look related, but I just don't see how they can be."

"Do people put those things together? The dolls, I mean. If you liked to sew or something, would you get the parts all separately and put them together to sell or collect? Like a kit." Max was looking at Camille with a direct gaze, and she found herself momentarily distracted by the lovely color of his eyes.

"I guess you can," she said, looking down at her hands so that he couldn't see her blush. "But Monica was a painter, not a craft person."

"What did Danni say about the heads?" he asked, plainly still puzzled.

"I actually didn't show them to her." Camille sighed and stretched out her legs slowly. "I thought she had too much on her mind already to be worried about them. And they really did spook me. I bagged them in Monica's bedroom and left them there. I guess we can figure out what to do with them tomorrow."

"I want to see them," Max said, rising from the couch.

"I thought you were taking me for some lunch," Camille said frowning. "I'm starved."

Max laughed and put out his hand for hers. As he pulled her to

122

Rachael Rawlings

her feet, he said lightly, "Fine, we'll eat today and think about this. Then tomorrow, if the doll's heads are still there, you can show them to Danni and I. It may be nothing. But it is just so strange," he left out the rest, but Camille could see how it added a twist. There was no reason a woman would pack china dolls' heads in her shoes and stow them in her closet. It made no sense.

~*~

After lunch, Max returned Camille safely to her apartment with a parting kiss on the cheek. Camille blushed and sighed like a school girl behind the closed door after he left, and then shook herself for her obvious crush on her neighbor. She wasn't sure when her feelings had changed, but in some ways, it made her happy, and that was worth a lot for her.

In the evening, she opened a bottle of wine and made her single eatable dish, spaghetti with a jarred sauce and freshly grated parmesan cheese. She toasted bread and listened in amusement as Simon imitated the sound of the toaster, the squeak of the back door opening, and a few bars of music from a soap commercial. As he was eating his fair share, she cleaned up the mess and turned on the news. The apartment was quiet, and she was still enjoying the buzz of emotions that Max's visit had left.

When the knock sounded at the door, she approached it with caution. She knew Max was working night shift that Leo had a date with his new girl, and that Danni may or may not be in the building. One look out the peep hole had her blood slipping from her fingertips and a chill racing down her spine. It was Mr. Tower. He was dressed impeccably in a suit and tie, and his hair was smoothed in a perfect uniform wave. She was thinking seriously about pretending he wasn't there, and hiding out in her bedroom, when his voice filtered in through the thin panel.

"I'm looking for Camille. I need to talk to you. Danni sent me."

Danni! How did he know Danni? Had he found her in Monica's apartment? Had they argued? Had he hurt her?

"What do you want?" her voice was not as stern as she had hoped, but it didn't waver either.

"Just to talk. Danni just left, and I wanted to talk to you now."

123

The Parrot Told Me

"This may not be a good time," Camille responded, her fingers hard and cold against the panel of the door as she looked back out into the hallway through the hole.

"I'm sorry, but I'm leaving town tomorrow with my family and I need to talk to you now. I would really prefer this not be through the door where everything can be heard."

Reluctantly, Camille opened the door, but blocked his entrance with her body. "My friend is due here in about ten minutes," she lied, her voice nice and calm. "You have that long."

He nodded, his handsome face looking older in the poor light. Or perhaps it was more than just lighting. "Can I come in?"

Camille stood back and let him in the door, but left the door ajar and did not sit down, even when he dropped into one of the kitchen chairs.

"You knew Monica," he said at last, his eyes landing on Simon who was perched on the top of the cage, his silver/gold eye appraising the man before him.

"Yes," Camille said cautiously.

"Then you knew about our relationship." His voice was flat and tired.

"Yes," Camille agreed, not adding any information.

Simon let out a mournful hoot. He shifted his weight and came to the side of the cage top. To Camille's surprise, Mr. Tower stood and went to the cage, bending to look Simon in his eye. With a practiced movement, he raised his hand, and when Simon ducked his head, he gently ruffled the feathers on the nape of his neck.

"Poor old Simon. Must be missing her, huh?" His voice was soft and Camille recognized the wheedling tone. His was the voice that Simon had imitated in the conversation. No doubt. Fear prickled up her back and slid up her scalp, making her shiver. "What happened to our girl?" he softly asked the bird. After a moment, he turned and looked at Camille. "I don't know what Monica told you, but I want you to know the truth. She did break it off with me, and I was not happy. I wasn't going to leave my family for her, but I didn't want to lose her either." He smiled bitterly. "One of those things where you want the best of both worlds and end up with nothing."

Camille had edged closer to the door, feeling the need for the possibility of escape.

"But Monica was wrong about one thing. I did care for her, and I would have continued to try to help her. I was supporting her painting until she started making it on her own, and I wasn't going to let them kick her out of her home."

"Monica didn't say anything about that." Camille was almost talking to herself.

"Monica was worried that she would lose the apartment, and she thought it was the only place that she could paint. She was so determined that everything had to stay the same. She could only paint if she used the same paint, same brushes, had the same light, same music." He stopped, his eyes angry, yet sad. "I know you must have seen the painting. I know you were in the apartment and must have seen my portrait."

Camille nodded, unable to lie. "Yes," she said softly. "It was beautiful."

Tower's smile was slow and sad. "It was. I took it. I had already told my wife, but I didn't want it coming out to the public, and her to have to suffer for it. I destroyed that painting."

"And your wife?"

"Is angry. She may let it go. I don't know. But I wanted you to know what I did. I didn't want you asking around about me anymore. I didn't want you searching for that painting. What was between Monica and I died before she ever did, and I don't want it hurting my family or hers."

Camille nodded mutely, still standing by the open door. Tower turned back to the bird and gave him a final scratch. With no further words, he walked out the door and strolled down the hallway, looking for all the world like the owner of the building, the owner of the world. What more did he have to lose? He had told his wife. He had lost his lover. He had destroyed the only evidence of his love. Not even Monica herself could have changed those things.

The Parrot Told Me

Chapter 13

The next morning at ten, Max, Danni, and Camille sat at her kitchen table eating breakfast sandwiches and making plans for the day. The truck was to arrive at two; the last of the boxes would be loaded and gone by then.

Danni had called the studio about Monica's work, and they had agreed to see her on Monday. They were not willing to guarantee that the show would still go on, but they would at least listen to Danni. Camille and Max were determined to help Danni choose some of the best pieces to take to the show, since no one could find a list of the works that Monica had planned on displaying. If it were up to Camille, the paintings would be shown, and in her stead, Danni would be there to represent Monica and her brilliance.

"I can't tell you how much I appreciate this," Danni said as they cleared their garbage and poured a second cup of coffee.

"Not a problem," Max replied, his eyes still a little weary. Camille knew he had worked all night on the giant airliners and had gotten little to no sleep between his shift and their meeting. But they would need his strength, and Camille was selfish enough to want him just for his company alone. "You all have done most of the hard parts. I didn't want to be on the cleaning crew."

Danni chuckled, her eyes less shadowed. "I won't ask for any real cleaning just yet. But if you make any mistakes, you get to scrub the sink."

Max nodded, his hand going to his ball cap in a small salute, "Yes, ma'am."

They went upstairs together, the spring air blowing generously through the window they threw open, blowing in with it the warm sun. The apartment felt empty now. Even full of furniture, it was lacking the essential Monica character that had made it different. Danni looked around with satisfaction. "It hasn't been too bad, thanks to all of your help," she said, looking toward Max and Camille.

"Did you happen to meet any more of Monica's friends when you were working up here?" Camille asked, thinking of Mr. Tower's visit. She hadn't had a chance to say anything to Max about her frightening evening, but was anxious to see if Tower had actually talked to Danni.

"Several, actually. I met your landlady who seemed pretty anxious for me to leave, and one of the neighbors from down your hall on the second floor," she said, looking meaningfully at Camille.

"Chloe?" Camille asked, her eyebrows raised automatically. "Talkative, full figured, blond."

Max grinned but didn't comment.

"Sounds like her. She was very friendly." Danni was too kind to complete the statement, but Camille nodded in understanding. "And I met Monica's boss. It was really nice that he came here."

Camille's eyes met Max's and he looked momentarily puzzled, then furious. He knew that Tower was a threat. He knew that the man was not safe, and possibly a murderer. His hand snaked out and he caught Camille's hand too tightly.

"Hey, Danni, let me borrow Camille for a second. I have something I want to show her in my apartment."

Danni smiled and nodded, turning back into the apartment while Max drug Camille into the hallway and through the unlocked front door of his own space.

Camille had never been in his apartment before, and she stood still, her eyes widening in amazement. If her apartment was cozy and quaint, his was the austere more sophisticated version. His furniture was only the finest antiques, his electronics, state of the art and kept on antique book cases, and his kitchen an array of cooking utensils that could have been part of a television cooking show.

"Wow," Camille murmured. "What did you say you did?"

"I rob little old ladies. You are off the topic. You knew that Tower was here. Did he come see you?"

"Yes. Yes, and I was going to tell you today. He stopped by and wanted to talk to me. I kept the door open and let him have his say."

Max raked his hand through his hair, his tired eyes looking irritated now. "You let him in your apartment?"

"Leo said that exact thing to me about the time I let you in,"

The Parrot Told Me

Camille said darkly. "I left the door open and stayed by the hall the whole time."

"Leo was right to worry. You need to be careful. You knew that man wasn't safe."

"I took precautions. Do you want to hear about what he said?"

At Max's irritated nod, she recounted Tower's story, and what he had said about Monica and their relationship. "But I know that it was his voice that Simon was imitating. I recognized it when he stopped talking like he was selling me something, and he went to pet Simon. His voice was really different. But Simon knew him and wasn't afraid. I don't know what that means either."

Max sighed and rubbed his eyes. "Just promise me this. Don't let that guy in unless you call me first. Don't let anyone in unless you call me first."

"Anyone?"

Max nodded, his face serious. "Now let's check with Danni. I don't like her to be alone either."

~*~

Back in the apartment, they didn't find Danni in the kitchen or living room, and Camille walked somewhat cautiously into the back bedroom. Danni was standing in the middle of the room, leaning against the footboard of Monica's bed. Her face was pensive.

"Are you okay?" Camille asked, drawing close.

Danni nodded and looked around. There were still a stack of boxes against the wall, but the rest of the room was bare. "Let's get started, then," Danni said briskly, pushing her mood away with an effort.

Camille nodded and they began picking up boxes and hauling them out into the hallway. From there they took trips going down the elevator with full loads and then reversed the pattern, taking out the boxes and laying them by the mailboxes near the door on the first floor. When Danni got the car and pulled it around, they filled it until it could hold no more. Danni took the car to the Salvation Army store by herself while Camille and Max went back upstairs to finish going through the bags and boxes.

"Where is the bag with the doll's heads?" Max asked when they returned to the apartment.

Camille gestured for him to follow her and scooped up the bag. They sat on the floor, and Camille fished in the bag, pulling out one of the paper wrapped parcels. When she rolled the head out onto her palm, Max visibly flinched.

"Not a fan," he said making a face. Camille passed it to him and watched as he studied it intently. While he looked at one, she unwrapped another, staring into its shiny blue eyes, its cupid lips permanently pinched in a kiss. The head was unchipped and looked new. The finish was perfectly shiny.

"Are these things supposed to be hollow?" Max asked, flipping the head over and looking into the neck.

"I don't know. This one isn't. Is yours?"

"This is not mine," he responded distastefully. "But this looks solid. It's chalky. You know, people smuggle drugs into the county in lots of different things."

"You think Monica was smuggling drugs in doll's heads?" Camille could hear the denial in her tone.

"I don't know, but it's a thought. Mara acted like Camille had some dangerous friends, and drug dealers would definitely be in that category."

"Let's put these away before Danni gets back," Camille said frowning. "Do you think we should go to the police?"

Max rubbed his prickly chin and sighed. "If these are just regular china doll's heads, we'd look like a couple of conspiracy theorists. We need a second opinion before we take these in."

"Know any drug lords?" Camille asked, playfully, wrapping the doll's head in the paper again.

"No," Max responded, but he was smiling. "But I do have some friends in security at the airport. They can help us with this." He stood quickly, the head still wrapped in his hand. "Let's get these out of here. I'll take a few in tonight or tomorrow and see what they come up with."

"Where do you want to keep the rest?" Camille asked, picking up the bag.

"I'd rather it not be with you. If someone has any idea that these exist, assuming they are what we think they are, someone will be coming after them."

The Parrot Told Me

"Oh, I doubt that," Camille said wryly, but she didn't volunteer to take the bag.

"I'm going to put this in my apartment. You wait here for Danni. We will leave this out until we know a little more."

Camille nodded and went back into the master bedroom. Mentally she scanned the room, looking for anything else needed to be cleared before the furniture would be taken away. She walked into the master bath, a soft sigh escaping her lips. She studied the tub, stripped of linens and curtain, the cabinet, empty now, and the outlet that had turned deadly. She felt sure that it hadn't been an accident. Someone had come into the bathroom and dropped that radio into the tub, using enough force and stealth that Monica hadn't had a chance to save herself. She felt shivers slid up and down her arms and she hugged herself. So had it been the jilted Mr. Towers? Some mysterious drug dealer? She stood still in the silence. Did Simon really know the answer?

She heard Max reenter the apartment and stepped back out into the bedroom to meet him. "Danni is pulling up the car. We can start getting the rest together if you want. The moving van is due in about thirty minutes."

Camille nodded, her thoughts miles away. She felt slightly defeated. Would they ever figure this out, especially with all of the evidence being shipped out by their own hands?

When Danni came in, they had put on cheerful expressions and were working on the second load to go to charity. The piles of trash had grown as well, and they started hauling out bags into the hallway. The sound of the elevator rising had Camille lifting her eyes from her task in the hallway, and she watched warily as Mrs. Patterson strolled down the hallway, her flat heeled shoes making a distinct clatter.

"What are you doing up here?" she asked coldly, her eyes going from Camille to the open apartment door.

"I was helping Danni move Monica's things out," Camille said stiffly, her mind shifting from the wrapped dolls' heads to the hideous collection in Mrs. Patterson's parlor.

"I wasn't aware that you knew each other."

Camille didn't reply, but nodded stiffly.

Mrs. Patterson frowned and turned back down the hallway, her pace slightly faster.

130

She stopped a moment later and looked back at Camille. "Where are all of these things going?" she asked, her voice loud enough to be heard clearly down the hall.

Camille just shrugged. It wasn't really any of Mrs. Patterson's business what Danni chose to do with the things. Besides, Mrs. Patterson seemed strange. She hadn't gone in the apartment, hadn't said a word to Danni, and hadn't even scolded them for the mess in the hallway. Camille shook her head and went back into the living room, still feeling uneasy.

~*~

Camille had hugged Danni tightly as she prepared to leave, feeling the other woman's grief. Danni had not bothered to hide her tears.

"I'll call you about the art show," Danni said, her voice rough with feeling. "I can't tell you how much I appreciate all of this." She ran her slender fingers through her hair.

Camille nodded. "I will be there. I wouldn't miss Monica's show after this." Nothing would keep her away now. "Let me know when you get home. I want to hear how your trip goes," she said, giving her new friend a forced smile. Then she had stood on the corner until Danni's car took the final turn out of sight.

Leo was over for the evening, and he met her on the stairs. It had been two days since they had finished packing Monica's apartment, and the professional cleaners had already been in. The apartment would be advertised in the next week's paper, and rented that fast.

"Danni got off alright?" he asked.

"She's fine," Camille responded, following him up the stairs. Their dinner of takeout pizza was laid out on the table, and Leo had added napkins and plates.

"So have you heard anything about the drugs?" Leo asked, pulling off one gooey slice and putting it on the china plate.

"No, Max hasn't seen his friend and doesn't want to haul them around in his truck just in case they are full of something illegal."

"So you are just waiting?" he asked, his brows rising, "must be hard for you."

Camille shrugged. "I've had a lot on my mind lately. I guess 'm just trying to keep things in perspective."

The Parrot Told Me

"How are you doing? About your sister, I mean?"

"I dream about her. I think about her a lot. I don't know. I guess it will get easier, but right now the timing seems..." she struggled with the word. Would she have handled the situation with Monica differently if her sister hadn't been the ghost in her past?

Leo put one hand loosely on hers, his fingers warm. She looked up and smiled gratefully.

"So let's change the subject. I got this great book in today, and I think it's going to sell well."

They talked shop through dinner, and put their paper plates in the garbage, stopping to open Simon's cage and let him wander across the top. He took a few crusts with a grateful whistle, and when they went in the other room, began his various discussions with himself, including squeaking doors, microwave beeps, and the phone ringing.

After a moments debate as to which wine they wanted to share, Camille went back into the kitchen to get some white wine and glasses, balancing Oreos in one arm. Leo was at her stereo, frowning. He pushed the button and music poured out, sweet.

Immediately, Simon started screaming, his voice rough and hysterical. The dialogue began just after, Monica's voice coming soft and sultry. The bird screams were first, then the threat, Tower's voice, and Monica begging to be let go. The dialogue continued, a copy of what they had already heard, and then the noise. Next, the sound of an angry Tower, "I'm leaving, but when I see you tomorrow, we are going to talk about this," and the perfect imitation of the door slam. Camille stood in frozen silence as the conversation closed, and the bird stood still. When Leo bent to turn off the music, Camille silently held up a finger, begging him to wait. A full throated gurgle of water was the next sound, the heavy sound of water pouring from a faucet, and the squeal of metal on metal, a shower curtain being pushed aside.

"What do you want?" Monica's tone was angry.

"I want the dolls!"

~*~

Leo sat next to Camille and poured her a second glass of wine. Her skin felt clammy, but the wine was warming her up gradually.

"I never thought it really was the dolls," Camille said softly. "I really thought it was Tower. A love thing."

Leo topped his own glass. "But Max has the dolls, and he will be taking care of them."

"Yeah," Camille said softly. "But I couldn't tell the voice. Did you recognize it?"

Leo shook his head. "It was deep, but it could have been a man or a woman." He swirled the golden liquid in his glass. "You out of Oreos?"

"I think so," Camille responded, and went into the kitchen. She pulled open the cabinets, eyeing Simon as she went. He was calm now. They had turned off the music, and although Camille was tempted to pitch the CD into the trash, Leo had refused and put it with his jacket. Camille didn't hear the apartment door open, or the struggle from the other room over the drone of the TV. When she turned, Mrs. Patterson was just there.

"You startled me," Camille breathed, her hand over her heart. Her mind couldn't seem to grasp it. Mrs. Patterson, standing in the doorway of her kitchen, one hand at her side. She had a fireplace poker. It wasn't Camille's, so she could only assume it had come from Mrs. Patterson's apartment. It was oddly shiny. Dripping. It was dripping something black on her hardwood floors.

"I want the dolls, and I'll leave you alone." Mrs. Patterson's voice was flat and even. "I didn't kill your friend, but if he doesn't get to the hospital soon, he will die. You need to tell me where the dolls are right now. Then I'll let you take him."

"Leo!" Camille found herself moving toward the door, unable to grasp that Mrs. Patterson, in her practical shoes and papery face, had just hurt Leo. Mrs. Patterson raised the poker, its shiny tip now in focus. Blood. Camille stepped back, away from the woman with the flat eyes.

"Camille, get me the dolls, and I will let you go to him."

Camille shook her head slowly. "But I don't have them." Her mind was beginning to clear. "They aren't here."

"I know that you were helping Danni to pack Monica's things, and I know that Danni doesn't have them, so that leaves you."

Camille's brain was starting to buzz and she saw the picture more clearly. She saw herself in the hall, carrying bags, telling Mrs. Patterson

The Parrot Told Me

that she was helping Danni. Mrs. Patterson had never seen Max. She didn't know anything about his involvement. But he had the dolls' heads in his apartment. If Mrs. Patterson knew that, she would go after him. But what of Camille and Leo? What of Max? Would Mrs. Patterson be willing to let any of them go?

"I'll give them to you after I see that Leo is okay," she said, her voice rough and strained.

Mrs. Patterson shook her head. "I'll take you to Leo after you give me what is mine." She moved toward Camille, the poker still raised. "It doesn't work the other way."

"They aren't here," Camille said truthfully. "I didn't want to keep them here in case they were dangerous."

Mrs. Patterson shook her head, her expression still blank, still frightening. "I think I can convince you to be honest," she said tightly. Before Camille even thought to move, the poker raised and as Camille threw up her arm to protect her face, the heavy metal instrument landed on her forearm with a dull crack. Blood sprayed onto Camille's face as the cruel barb punctured the skin, and she dropped to her knees. She automatically cradled the arm against her abdomen as the pain moved in her like a current of white hot electricity.

"Do you want to tell me now?" Mrs. Patterson's face was composed and expressionless.

Camille sagged on the floor, her face feeling numb. She wondered if she was going to pass out, there on the hardwood with her unprotected friend in the other room.

"What the hell," the sound came from the cage, but the voice was Monica's.

Mrs. Patterson's face registered shock, and she turned toward the sound.

"What do you want?" the voice came again.

"Damn bird," Mrs. Patterson screeched, approaching the cage, the poker forgotten in her hand.

Camille could see Simon, his feathers puffed and eyes pinning, coming to the side of the top of the cage in defense. As Mrs. Patterson approached, he stood stiffly, still and waiting. He eyed her, still trembling slightly.

"I'll wring your neck," Mrs. Patterson said, her eyes not quite sane. "Like a chicken," she spat, ducking forward.

The bird moved immediately, razor sharp beak and claws at level with Mrs. Patterson's face. The bird was screaming, and Mrs. Patterson's cries could barely be heard over the sound, the sound of the bird and then the sound of steady pounding on the door. The apartment door finally gave from the weight of the blows, and Max rushed in, followed by two strangers in uniform. Camille said his name in a soft cry, and fell forward in a faint.

~*~

"Hey, there." Max's face was close, his fingers warm on her forehead. "It's alright now. She's already gone, and the ambulance is coming. They took Leo first."

"Leo," she said, her voice breaking.

"Has a hard head. He's going to have to have a new hairstyle for a while, but the EMT didn't suspect a fracture."

"Where is he?"

"Gone. The first ambulance checked him out and took him. He'll be at the hospital when you get there."

Camille became aware of the bustle of men laying out a stretcher.

"You ready?" Max said, and looked up at the EMT.

"Yeah, we're good, but you're going to have to move that bird. We can't take it with us, and it looks kind of mean."

Max smiled and glanced down. Camille followed his gaze and saw Simon, scruffy and puffed, perched on her leg at the knee. "He hasn't left you. He let them put on the bandage, but he's lunged at anyone who gets too close."

"Simon," she said softly. "My hero."

"We all saw Mrs. Patterson's face. None of us want to get him mad again."

"Help me sit up," Camille requested softly. Max gently eased her shoulders up, stopping momentarily while she got her breath. He nudged her up a few inches more until she could put out her good hand. "Come here, Simon, step up."

The bird stepped to her hand, his eyes focused on her face. He tilted his head and looked at her carefully, letting out a low mournful

The Parrot Told Me

whistle. Slowly she held him out to Max, and he stepped onto Max's outstretched hand. When the EMTs transferred her to the stretcher, Max rose and placed Simon into his cage.

"Make sure a vet checks him out," she asked Max softly. "He saved my life."

~*~

In the hospital, Camille lay in the soft cushion of medication. Her arm had needed surgery, but Leo was stable and had woken for a brief time. He had even made a joke to Max about his shaven head, so Max declared that he was as good as new. Max had ridden with her to the hospital, and his two uniformed friends, security from the airport, had followed. They would help sort out the story with the police.

Camille turned her head slowly and looked at her mother. Her mother looked pale, her clothes rumpled and her hair slightly mussed, but relaxed. When Camille's eyes fluttered open, she smiled.

"How are you feeling now?" Camille's mother asked, her voice pitched low.

"Okay," Camille lied. "Have you seen Leo?"

"He's resting, but he's going to be fine." Camille's mom moved to the head of the bed. "Your dad is out talking to the police. Your neighbor Max has some of his security friends with him, and they are talking about what that woman did."

"Good," Camille said softly. She was feeling foggy again, but struggling to stay awake. "Have you heard about Simon?"

Camille's mom gently took her good hand. "Max took him to a vet."

"What vet?"

"I called Mara," Max said from the doorway. "I figured it was the least she could do. She knew the vet that Monica went to with Simon and gave me the name." He walked into the room and stood at the foot of the bed. "When I called the vet and told them about what Simon had done. Thank God they offered to come and get him. I don't think he would have let me touch him again. But he looked fine. Mean, but fine." Max smiled slightly. "They called me a few minutes ago and said that his health looks good, he might have broken a blood feather or

136

something, but they are keeping him overnight."

Camille's mom sighed. "Can you rest now? When you wake up, you'll have some explaining to do."

Camille felt like a child when her mother looked at her like that. "I'm sorry, Mom. I didn't want to worry you."

"You're fine now, and that's all that matters."

Camille felt a heavy fatigue wash over her, chased by the medication swirling in her veins. Max came to her side and leaned over close, his warm breath against her forehead.

"I'll be here when you wake up. We did a good thing, here. I know that Monica would agree." His lips brushed her cheek and she closed her eyes, finally at rest. She heard him dimly as she sunk under the wave of sedation. "And I owe that bird a big favor."

The Parrot Told Me

Acknowledgment:

I will first thank God, who has provided me the wonderful world in which to live. The miracles of nature, of the creatures all around me, are a constant source of entertainment, comfort, and joy.

I would also like to thank my wonderful publisher, Tony Acree; my editor, Julie Gabis; and all the authors at Hydra Publications for their support, ideas, and encouragement.

And, of course, I thank my family for standing by me, putting up with me, and listening to my crazy ideas. I especially thank my daughter, Faith, who provided the draft of my cover as well as company on some of my book trips.

And lastly, thanks to my readers for letting me have a little bit of your time and imagination.

About the author:

Rachael Rawlings is a full time mother, wife, writer, pet owner, and Speech Language Pathologist. Her main goal is to show readers a good time, make them think a little, and make them wonder and marvel about things that are all around us.

She lives with her husband, James, a professional architect; her three children, Faith, Nicholas, and Chase; and two dogs. She is also owned by two parrots who continually surprise her in their sheer intelligence (a new definition of bird brained). She grew up and lives in the small town of Crestwood, Kentucky.

She thrives on good coffee, chocolate, and great friends and family. To learn more about Rachael's work and her upcoming releases, visit her on her website:

http://rachaelrawlings.wix.com/rachael-rawlings

The Parrot Told Me

CPSIA information can be obtained at www.ICGtesting.com
Printed in the USA
BVOW06s1634290715

410990BV00014B/111/P